SHOLEM ASCH
UNDERWORLD
TRILOGY

SHOLEM ASCH
UNDERWORLD TRILOGY

GOD OF VENGEANCE
MOTKE THIEF
THE DEAD MAN

TRANSLATED BY CARAID O'BRIEN

For rights/production permission contact
www.caraidobrien.com
caraidobrien@gmail.com

White Goat Press, the Yiddish Book Center's imprint
Amherst MA 01002

Book and cover design by Michael Grinley

ISBN 979-8-9871609-9-2
Library Of Congress Control Number 2023905482

Printed at The Studley Press, Dalton, MA

WHITE
GOAT
PRESS

whitegoatpress.org

TABLE OF CONTENTS

TRANSLATOR'S INTRODUCTION

Sholem Asch is one of the most translated and performed Yiddish playwrights in history. His *Underworld Trilogy* is three separate plays— *god of vengeance* (1907), *Motke Thief* (1917), and *The Dead Man* (1922). *god of vengeance* and *Motke Thief* take place in the criminal underworld, and *The Dead Man* unfolds in the actual underworld—the land of the dead. All three works were successfully produced on the Yiddish stages of America and Europe, and their influence continues to be felt throughout the theater world today.

God of vengeance remains one of the most well-known plays of the Yiddish theater, the story of a brothel owner, whose daughter has a lesbian affair with a prostitute, trying to buy his way into respectability. I first encountered the play in Yiddish in a class with Ruth Wisse in 1995. When I saw my first English-language production of the play a few years later, I was shocked by how completely it was divorced from the power and energy of the original. Encouraged by my collaborator Aaron Beall, I translated it anew, and we produced it on the go-go stage at the infamous Show World strip club in Times Square in 1999.

Next, I turned my attention to *Motke Thief*, a psychological portrait of a gangster set among Warsaw's criminal class, which includes some of the same characters as *god of vengeance*, including the pimp Shlomo and his charges Basha and Rayzl. We staged the production at University Settlement in 2005. One production of *Motke Thief* in the 1920s at Maurice Schwartz's Art Theater brought the Academy Award–winning actor Paul Muni, then known as Muni Weisenfreund, to the attention of Broadway producers.

In 2019 I received a grant from the Yiddish Book Center to translate four more Sholem Asch plays, among them *The Dead Man*, the third play in Asch's *Underworld Trilogy*. The underworld in *The Dead Man* is not the world of criminals but rather the world of the dead. A soldier crosses back over into the land of the living to bring his fiancée back with him to the other side. I adapted the play as a one-act in 2003, and we staged it at the Eldridge Street Synagogue. This latest version, however, is a complete translation of the entire script. *The Dead Man* successfully premiered in Chicago in 1922, where it received a rave review from future Hollywood screenwriter Ben Hecht, who later quoted the play in his script for the 1938 movie version of Emily Bronte's novel *Wuthering Heights*. Set in the flu epidemic of 1919, we recorded it as a radio play during the coronavirus epidemic of 2021 for Carnegie Hall's Voice of Hope Festival.

These three plays represent just a small fraction of Sholem Asch's theatrical output. He wrote over two dozen dramas, and many of his novels, including *Motke Thief*, were adapted for the stage by himself and others. He was the most produced playwright at Maurice Schwartz's legendary Yiddish Art Theater, a Lower East Side institution that boasted 3,000 seats and is now a Loew's movie house, and the first playwright ever produced by the world famous Vilna Troupe.

A major part of my translation process is working with actors. A script isn't finished until actors have performed it, and changes are always made until the very last moment. It is with deep gratitude to the dozens of actors who worked with us on these texts over the past twenty years that we are able to offer you these plays to read and perform today. Each play includes an introduction and a glossary of Yiddish words used in performance. I'd also like to thank my translation mentor, Linda Gaboriau, who worked with me on *The Dead Man* during my translation fellowship. And lastly, none of my work would have been possible without the influence, teaching, and theatrical memory of my two beloved acting teachers, Luba Kadison, the last surviving member of the Vilna Troupe, who starred in *god of vengeance* as Rivkele opposite Stella Adler's *Manke*, and Seymour Rexite, the golden-voiced tenor of the Yiddish stage, former president of the Hebrew Actors Union, and radio historian of the Yiddish theater. Luba taught me about the Yiddish literary theater and Seymour educated me in the history of the Yiddish musical. I met with them both weekly from 1997 until their deaths in 2006 and 2002 respectively. May their spirits live on in future productions of these plays!

—Caraid O'Brien

GOD OF VENGEANCE

INTRODUCTION TO *GOD OF VENGEANCE*

Sholem Asch remains one of the most controversial Broadway playwrights in American theater history, yet he never wrote a play in English. In the early 1920s, two years before Mae West was thrown into the slammer for jumping into bed with sailors in her racy farce *Sex*, Rudolph Schildkraut starred in an English translation of Asch's *god of vengeance*, a drama about a Jewish brothel owner who attempts to go legit by commissioning a Torah scroll and marrying off his daughter to a yeshiva student. After a six-week run on Broadway, the entire cast spent a night in jail charged with "lewd behavior" for performing in what was Asch's first full-length play, complete with Jewish prostitutes, a lesbian scene, and a Torah hurled across the stage.

Born in Kutno, Poland, in 1880 into a large Orthodox Jewish family, as a young man the budding writer abandoned his religious studies and spent a few years slumming in the Warsaw underworld before moving to America. One of his first jobs was writing letters for the illiterate—people from all walks of life, including criminals and prostitutes. This work, at which he surely excelled, gave him deep psychological insight into many different strata of society. Historically, artists and criminals have always lived side by side, poverty and unfettered ambition bringing them close together. It was this milieu that provided Asch with much of his early inspiration for the pimps and prostitutes of *god of vengeance*. He clearly preferred their company to the religious hypocrites he left behind.

Written by the former rabbinical student when he was about 26 years old, *god of vengeance* is a send-up of the typical bourgeoisie melodrama. The play opens with a precious mother-daughter scene as Soreh and Rivkele prepare the house for visitors, unremarkable except that this family lives above a brothel and Mother used to be a whore. The first act ends with Soreh describing her fantasy marriage for her daughter to a handsome yeshiva scholar, while behind her Rivkeleh begins passionately kissing one of the prostitutes from downstairs.

Asch has a great sympathy for his subjects, as well as an understanding for the limited opportunities available to them that lead to a life of crime and prostitution. Act two takes place in the brothel and is a deeply human portrait of the young women who live there. As the prostitute Basha says, explaining why she rejected a marriage with the local butcher, "I should go marry Shtinky and every year make another little Shtinky?"

In the scene that shut down the production, Manke and Rivkele cuddle and kiss together before Manke asks her to run away. Manke promises Rivkele that they will go to a place where "no one will hit her, no one will scream at her," where "they can sleep together the whole night in one bed." Everyone wants a piece of poor Rivkele, a young woman discovering her sexuality, unaware of her own vulnerability. Her parents want to use her to move up in society, Manke wants her as her lover, the older prostitute Hindl and her boyfriend Shlomo want to pimp her out, and Reb Eli wants to marry her off and collect his matchmaking commission.

The Daddy in *god of vengeance* dares to challenge God and his position in society. When Yankl realizes his daughter has been kidnapped he says, "Only I ask you, Rebbe—Why didn't God want me? Why didn't he bother to save you, Yankl Shapshovitch, from the swamp that sucks you down?" Ultimately, he rejects both God and respectable society after his daughter is corrupted in his eyes. As he says at the end of the play, abandoning all pretenses toward religion and hurling the sacred totem across the stage: "Take your Torah. I don't need it anymore."

God of vengeance had been a huge hit when it premiered in German in 1907 at the Deutsches Theater in Berlin, directed by one of the most celebrated directors of his day, Max Reinhardt, and starring the legendary actor Rudolph Schildkraut (father of the Academy Award–winner Joseph Schildkraut). A few years earlier Asch had seen Schildkraut star as Shylock in *The Merchant of Venice* and was inspired to write the part of Yankl Shapshovitch especially for him. *god of vengeance* was subsequently performed throughout the world in Russian, French, Polish, Dutch, Swedish, Norwegian, and Italian. It was also performed in New York City on Second Avenue in its original Yiddish beginning as early as 1907.

The infamous 1923 Broadway production, translated by Isaac Goldberg, marked the first time the play was performed in the United States in English. The play, again starring Schildkraut as the brothel owner, also launched the career of 23-year-old Morris Carnovsky, playing as his first Broadway role an elderly Biblical scribe. Despite a successful run at the Provincetown Playhouse in Greenwich Village and capacity houses for the duration of its interrupted Broadway showing, the production was shut down at the Apollo Theater on 42nd Street after only a few weeks. The play about a Jewish brothel owner and his attempt to become respectable was deemed immoral.

This revolt was led by Rabbi Silverman, a reform rabbi who was outraged by the portrayal of Jews on stage as pimps and prostitutes. The producer, star, and entire cast were jailed and prosecuted, resulting in fines of up to $500 each or a maximum three years in prison. They were charged with presenting an obscene and indecent play. Producer Harry Weinberger, also a lawyer, acted for the defense. In the ensuing trial, the jury deliberated for under an hour and found the entire company guilty. (The decision was overturned on appeal.)

When I first read the play in its original Yiddish, I found the script beautiful and poetic—culminating in the tender love scene between the two young women. But I was even more captivated by the gritty sexuality and vibrancy that characterized much of the dialogue. The fluid nature of Yiddish allows Asch to write an almost different vernacular for each personality—the more religious have a Hebraicized Yiddish, the country naïve a more Polish vocabulary, the criminal element uses a more Russified Yiddish, and so on. Although most of his characters are Jewish, their cultural, national, and ideological backgrounds are different, and it is this uniquely Jewish collision of cultures within a common ground that Asch captures in his writing. The scribe, the most religious character, speaks the most Hebrew phrases. Shlomo, the incorrigible young pimp, uses more Russian. The dialect Asch creates for each role is so specific and unique that his fully formed characters resonate deeply—because of their cultural specificity—with the universal in all cultures. Reading Asch's plays, one can see how the Jewish communities he creates are a microcosm for the class, religious, and moral divides existing across all cultures throughout the modern world.

In the late 1990s, I saw a production of the play in a translation that made Asch's script seem awkward and melodramatic, nothing like the masterpiece I had first read in Yiddish. On the urging of Todo con Nada's Aaron Beall, I decided to translate the play myself with the belief that this was one of the great works of the twentieth century.

This translation is not an adaptation; it is

a literal translation that stays as close to the text as possible. In our translations we look to imitate Asch's phrasing and diction as much as possible and to include a layer of the original Yiddish so as not to sever the play sonically from the cultural specificity of the source text. Yiddish words or phrases appearing in the translation are meant to emphasize very specific moments in the text and mark moments of intense or increasing emotion—during the love scene between Mankeh and Rivkeleh, for instance, Yiddish is used and then followed by its English equivalent, often because Asch repeats the phrase in his script.

I sense that translators sometimes feel the need to "improve" a play by adapting the script instead of treating it as a great work of art that should be seen first as the author originally intended. And some translations are completely divorced from the rhythms and sounds of their original Yiddish, creating a script that is not rooted in any particular culture, let alone the Jewish communities of Eastern Europe and America. Imagine if John Millington Synge's *The Playboy of the Western World* had been written without the cadence of Irish Gaelic beneath its Irish-language-peppered English text.

Once we completed several drafts, our translation of *god of vengeance* was then developed through performance, beginning with a run in Times Square just around the corner from where the cast of Goldberg's very fine translation was arrested in 1923. Because of Mayor Giuliani's zoning laws from the 1990s requiring porn shops to have at least 60 percent cultural programming, Show World—the world-famous porn emporium right across from Port Authority—was compelled to bring in "nonadult" entertainment to keep the video peep shows open. They were looking to book the go-go room, and all the girls had to be dressed. Aaron Beall, whose storefront theater Nada had led the artistic revitalization of Ludlow Street beginning in the late 1980s, heard about the venue and scheduled a meeting with

the owner of Show World. He wrote a plan to transform the second floor into a series of ninety-nine-seat theaters and rehearsal halls.

As a result, Beall's Obie Award–winning company Todo con Nada became the artists in residence, with *god of vengeance* among the first on the docket. Overnight we had a theater, complete with a pole, mirrored walls, and red and black décor, right on the edge of the theater district. The run, due in equal part to the notoriety of the play, the theater, and reputation of its performers and director, was sold out.

In addition to the Todo con Nada production at Show World, Theater J (Ari Roth, artistic director) and the Rorschach Theater (Jenny McConnell/Randy Baker) in Washington, DC, produced a run of this translation. And more recently the Yiddish Theatre Ensemble (Laura Sheppard/Bruce Bierman) in Berkeley produced a Zoom version of the script, with inventive set designs by Jeremy Knight. At the urging of Broadway producer Ted Tulchin, Douglas Carter Beane of the Drama Department cast a reading of the script with Billy Crudup as Shlomo, F. Murray Abraham as Yankl, Fiona Bishop as Soreh, and Emerie Snyder as Rivkele, who also played the role at Theater J.

We also had two priceless advisors working with us on the Show World production whose help and input was immeasurable: Luba Kadison and Seymour Rexite. Luba, a founding member of the Vilna Troupe, appeared in the original production of that most famous Yiddish play, *The Dybbuk*, in Warsaw in 1920. I met Luba my senior year at Boston University while writing an undergraduate paper on the visionary production of Osip Dimov's *Yoshke Musicant* she created with her husband Joseph Buloff in 1924 in Romania that influenced a young Eugene Ionescu.

Our second advisor was the president of the Hebrew Actors Union, the singer and former wunderkind Seymour Rexite. I interviewed Seymour many times while writing a Yiddish theater website for NYU, and he had given me my first-ever script to produce while I was managing a theater in the basement of the Lower East Side Tenement Museum. Seymour also introduced us to our publicist, Max Eisen, who had owned one of the original off-Broadway theaters, the Theater DeLyce; Max was the first publicist to get the *New York Times* to review off-Broadway shows and picketed *The New Yorker* for not listing Yiddish shows. We received great support from the press in Yiddish, German, and English. The script was excerpted in the National Foundation for Jewish Culture's *Jewish Culture News*. A picture of Mercedes McAndrew as Rayzl was on the front page of *The Forward*. *The Village Voice* wrote that this production of the play "set Show World aflame." *The Jewish Week* said "Their eyes were watching God." The gay weekly *The Blade* did a beautiful photo essay of the production that included several elderly Yiddishists holding their programs in the Show World lobby.

Aaron Beall, the creator of the New York International Fringe Festival, directed the show, interspersing sound and video elements from Ridley Scott's *Blade Runner* against the sleazy red and black mirrored décor and golden pole of the Show World go-go stage. After seventy-six years in exile, we felt thrilled to return *god of vengeance* to Times Square just around the corner from where the play premiered on Broadway at the Apollo Theater in 1923. We opened in one millennium and closed in another, and somehow that felt right.

TRANSLATOR'S NOTE
FOR *GOD OF VENGEANCE*

The transliterated Yiddish text is according to a standard Yiddish dialect. If the play is set in Poland at the turn of the century, a Polish Yiddish dialect can be used. The actors should *not* speak the English lines with a "Jewish" accent.

The Yiddish words or phrases appear at very specific moments in the text and mark moments of intense or increasing emotion—during the love scene between Manke and Rivkele, for instance, or Yankl's descent into madness during the third act. The scribe and Reb Eli speak more Yiddish than other characters because they are more religious. In short, if a character speaks Hebrew it is for a reason. When Shlomo calls Soreh *"a gute yidene"* in the third act, he is playing upon her attempt to become more religious. The language of each character, whether it be Yiddish, Russian, or American slang, exposes their individual backgrounds, in particular with regards to his or her "Jewishness."

The punctuation, including ellipses, is much as it appears in the original. The ellipses signify a change of thought or an intensity of emotion. They are intended to imitate the natural rhythms of speech and are not meant as pauses. We attempted to use YIVO orthography whenever possible when transliterating Yiddish names and words. Sometimes this became distracting, especially when the transliterated spelling has the same spelling as a random English word, as in *Sore*, which we spell as *Soreh*, and the word *kale* (bride), which we spell as *kaleh* to avoid an irrelevant association. For this same reason, we translate the word for *yes* as *yau*, not *yo*.

ORIGINAL CAST

First performance November 20, 1999, on the go-go stage at Todo con Nada Show World in Times Square, NYC

Yankl Shapshovitch	Mark Greenfield
Soreh	Andrea Darriau
Rivkeleh	Vered Hankin/Tonya Krohn
Mankeh	Elizabeth Gondek
Hindl	Caraid O'Brien
Shlomo	Corey Carthew
Rayzl	Mercedes McAndrew
Basha	Naomi Odes
Reb Eli	David Pincus
The scribe	Shane Baker
An unknown visitor	Shane Baker
Woman with one eye	Maux Kelly Nolan
Another poor woman	Lisa Szymanski
The poor	Shay Guttman, Noah Kay, James Henderson
	Naomi Odes, Irina, and others

A Todo con Nada production
Directed by Aaron Beall. Produced by Caraid O'Brien. Stage Manager: Troy Fuss. Assistant Stage Managers: Lisa Syzmanski, Mo Kelly Nolan. Set and Costumes: Enya Gonkova. Advisors: Seymour Rexite and Luba Kadison. Photographs: Russell/Martin, Julia Parshina. Publicity: Max Eisen. Film: Eli Diner. Graphic Design: Duck Rhattigan.

DRAMATIS PERSONAE

Yankl Shapshovitsh	The Daddy, boss of a brothel
Soreh	his wife, a former prostitute
Rivkele	his daughter, a young girl of 17
Hindl	the head prostitute, thirtysomething, on her way out
Manke	the second prostitute, still young
Rayzl	the third prostitute
Basha	a provincial girl, newly arrived, also a prostitute
Shlomo	a fop and aspiring pimp, Hindl's supposed fiancé, a good-looking man, 26
Reb Eli	a traditional matchmaker, a go-between for The Daddy
A scribe	handwrites a Torah scroll for Shapshovitsh
An unknown visitor	a potential father-in-law for Rivkele
An old woman	blind in one eye (one of the poor)
Another poor woman	
The poor	

Time	after 1907
Place	a Jewish city

ACT ONE

Scene: The Daddy's private dwellings on the ground floor of an old wooden house. Below in the cellar is a brothel. A flight of creaky wooden stairs announces all visitors and leads from outside into the home. At the rear is a door leading to the outside. To the right is a door to Rivkele's room. The finishing touches are being put on the cleaning of the house.

(Soreh, Rivkeleh, later the Daddy)

Soreh is tall and slim, a prepossessing woman; her features are coarsened, although they retain traces of her former beauty, which even now has a tone of insolence.

Rivkele *(a graceful young girl, neatly and modestly dressed)* *Ot azoy, Mameshi,* now I'm going to decorate the mirror. See, Mommy, doesn't this look pretty?

Soreh *(busy setting the table)* Hurry, *tokhtershi,* hurry, *Tate* has already gone out to the neighbors. They're going to help him bring the Sefer Torah home.

Rivkele It will be pretty. People will come . . . We will play and we will sing . . . *Yau, Mameshi?*

Soreh Yes, daughter dear. My life. This is a *khinekh.* It's a great mitzvah . . . It isn't everyone who can have a Sefer Torah written, who can pay a scribe to write by hand every sacred word of God. A real *balebos,* a distinguished man . . .

Rivkele And will other girls come too? Will we dance? Really, *Mameshi?* *(stops moving)* I must buy a new blouse, Mommy, and a pair of white pumps. *(sticks out her feet)* I can't dance in these boots, you know, *dokh.*

Soreh When you get engaged, *mirts-hashem* and become a *kaleh* this spring around Pesach, I will make you a long dress and I'll buy you a pair of white pumps. All the girls will come around, stylish girls from good families. You'll become friends with them.

Rivkele *(stubborn)* You always say, "Wait 'til Pesakh." I am already an adult. *(looks in the mirror)* Look, Mommy, I am already an adult. *(showing her hair)* Look how long my hair is. Manke says that . . . *(stops abruptly)* And Manke will be there, right, *Mameshi*?

Soreh No, daughter dearest. Only *balebatishe kinder*, young ladies . . . You are a *balebatish kind*, a young lady.

Rivkele Why not, Mother dearest? Manke drew King Dovid's crown on the Sefer Torah cover for me . . . I'm going to embroider it now with silk thread and decorate it with leaves and flowers, you'll see how pretty it will look, *Mameshi*, *(points to her embroidered pictures on the wall)* a hundred times better than those . . .

Soreh *(shocked)* *Vey iz mir*, don't tell your father. *Er vet shrayn. Tate* would be very angry.

Rivkele Why, Mommy? It's for the Torah, isn't it?

Soreh *Tate* will rave. *(she hears a step)* *Shvayg*, Rivkele, *Tate* is coming.

The Daddy *(still on the stairs, a tall dark man, a young-looking 40)* Why should I beg them . . . I have a real business. They won't come, who needs them . . . I've gathered together some poor people . . . Don't be afraid. We've got latkes with applesauce and slices of goose. *(sees Rivkele, sits)* Come to *Tate*, baby.

Soreh *(angry, hiding it by continuing to set the table)* They won't soil their *yikhes* with the likes of you, is that it? But if they need a hundred on credit . . . a charitable donation, they're not ashamed of you at all . . . The goy is *treyf*, but his cash is kosher . . .

The Daddy   What's biting her ass? Oh! Collecting new worries. Don't worry about it. Nothing will be spoiled . . . *(calls Rivkele)* Nu, *kum* here to *Tate*, baby.

Rivkele   *(unwilling, goes to her father, frightened)* What do you want, *Tateshi*?

The Daddy   Don't be scared, Rivkeh-baby, I won't do anything bad to you. *(takes her by the hand)* You love your *Tate, yau*?

Rivkele nods her head yes

The Daddy   Then why are you scared of *Tate*?

Rivkele   I don't know.

The Daddy   Don't be scared of your father; *Tate* has only love for you, a lot of love. Today, we're bringing home the Sefer Torah that I had written for you. It cost a lot of money. It's for you, my baby, for you.

Rivkele is silent

The Daddy   *Az got vet helfn* and you become a *kaleh*, I will buy your *khosn* a gold watch with a gold chain—that's a half pound of gold . . . Your *Tate* has a lot of love for you.

Rivkele is quiet, lowers her head

The Daddy   Don't be ashamed. You may become a *kaleh*, God said so. *(pause)* It's *gornisht*—nothing . . . Everyone becomes a wife or husband.
Rivkele is silent

The Daddy	*Nu*, do you love your *Tate*?
Rivkele	*(nodding her head) Yau*.
The Daddy	*Nu*—so, what do you want me to buy for you? Tell me Rivke-baby. *(Rivkele doesn't answer) Nu*, tell, don't be scared. Your *Tate* loves you. *Nu*, tell. What should I buy for you?

Rivkele is silent

Soreh	*(busy with the table; to Rivkele) Nu*-so, why don't you answer your *Tate* when he speaks to you?
Rivkele	I don't know . . .
Soreh	*(to The Daddy)* She wants a silk blouse with a pair of white pumps.
The Daddy	Ah, you want a silk blouse with a pair of white pumps?

Rivkele nods her head yes

The Daddy	It's yours. *(takes money out of his pocket and offers it to her) Yau*, give that to *Mameshi*, let her buy it for you.

Rivkele takes the money and gives it to her mother. There is noise on the stairs as the poor ready themselves to enter.

The Daddy	*(to Soreh)* See, and you said *(opens the door)* that you wouldn't have any guests. *(calls) Nu*, come in, *kumt arayn, kumt arayn. A crowd of poor people enter, men and women, first one by one as if they were sneaking in, then boldly in groups. All greet Yankl, some ironically.*
The poor	*Gut morgn* to you Patron, *Baltsedoke, (to Soreh)* and a good day to you Madame, *baleboste*.

Soreh puts food in apron and passes it around to the guests.

One of the poor   May you have a long life, *baleboste*, so that you can enjoy many more joyous *simkhes* like this one.

A woman blind in one eye   The Sefer Torah will bring you success and be a blessing on your home . . .

The Daddy   *(throwing slices of bread at the poor people; to Soreh)* Give them a pound of latkes each with extra applesauce. Let everyone have a little bottle of whiskey to take home. They should know that today in my house is a *simkhe* . . . *Nishkoshe*, I can afford it.

A woman blind in one eye   *(praising Soreh and Yankl in front of everybody)* This is some house, like no other. What a year I've had already. Nobody leaves this place emptyhanded. A cup of soup for the sick, a shirt for a poor man. What then do you get from the other *balebatim?*—Nothing, 'cept a view of their high windows . . .

Soreh, as if she does not hear the woman, throws more food in the blind woman's lap. The woman holds up her apron and continues.

A woman blind in one eye   Here, when they have a little party, excuse me, a *simkhe* . . . you can be who you want . . . You can shake it with the best of them . . .

Another poor person   *(among the others)* Such a year already on us, such a year already on us . . .

The Daddy   *(takes out some small change and gives it to Rivkele)* *Nu*, divide this up among the poor people. *(Rivkele passes out the change)*

A woman blind in one eye   *(with more feeling, turns to Rivkele)* And show me in the entire city a more modest young lady . . . *(to the other women)* Rebbes don't even have such children. *(softly yet loudly enough so the hosts* *can hear) Un Got veyst* where they got such a kosher kid . . . Imagine, to grow up in a such a house, may God not punish me for saying it . . . *(louder)* And they mind her like the *oyg* in their own head. They measure her every step. It warms my belly just to look at her. *(goes over to Yankl) Nishkoshe*, let them hear it. *(looks at Rivkele)* If I had a son, a rebbe, I'd give him her for his *kaleh*.

Another woman	*(among the others)* Let them hear it . . . Let them hear it . . .
The Daddy	You'll be there to see it when I carry this little one to the wedding *khupe*! A whole goose for every one of you, and a live pike fish as well—and a sack of money on top of it or my name isn't Yankl Shapshovitsh if I'm telling a lie . . .
The woman blind in one eye	Let me tell you it's as if she was raised in a synagogue, a shul, *l'havdil* . . . Clean . . . Pretty . . . As modest as any rebbe's *tokhter* . . .
The other women	Let them hear it . . . Let them hear it . . .
The Daddy	*(passing out the glasses of whiskey to the poor, lets slip out a word before catching himself)* Even though her father is Yankl Shapshovitsh . . .
Soreh	*(passing out glasses) Nu-nu*, look at himself, bragging to that lot.
The Daddy	*(pouring whiskey in the glasses unrestrained, speaking passionately as he passes out the glasses)* It makes no difference to me if you're poor or rich. Everyone should know it . . . Let the entire city know it . . . I am what you say I am. *(looking at his wife)* What she is—she is. Everything is true, everything . . . But I'll not let one word fall against my child . . . If not, I will, *ot*, I will split their head open with this bottle . . . I don't even care if it's the rebbe himself. It's all the same to me . . . My daughter

is more pure than his. *(pointing to his neck)* I'll let you cut into me right here.

Soreh *(stops what she's doing)* *Nu*, we've heard it already . . . Heard it already . . . *(claps her hands and looks for a broom)* We have to tidy up, chop, chop, the other *balebatim* will be here shortly. That's enough now. *(turning to the poor people)* You don't mind, do you?

The poor No, Mrs. Boss, *a gdule un nakhes af ayer kop*. Many more feathers for your cap missus . . . God bless you. *(they leave one by one, blessing everyone as they go)*

Soreh Go, Rivkele, and get the little skirt ready for the Sefer Torah. Reb Eli will be here any moment with the scribe.

Rivkele exits left to her room. Soreh remains alone with The Daddy, sweeping the room.

Soreh Who was he bragging to? They're nobodies. Freeloaders . . . Why wouldn't they come visit you? Make a *simkhe* every day, and you'll have them every day . . . In respectable homes, they know how to behave. They keep their distance, show respect for a human being. Then there's you. They're your best friends . . . What are you some drunken Russian? You're one hell of a respectable guy, I'll tell you that much, a real *balebos*.

The Daddy You want the neighbors to come to you? You have a face. There's a mirror. Have you forgotten who you are?

Soreh "Who you are?" What? Have you stolen anything? You have a business. Every man has his business. You've forced *dokh* nobody! . . . You can deal in whatever you want as long as you yourself do nothing wrong . . . Try and give them some money, then you'll see how much they'll take from you.

The Daddy   Oh, they'll take it from you, but they'll still see you as a dog . . . In shul, you'll stand by the door . . . They'll never give you an aliyah. They'll never call you up to read from the Torah . . .

Soreh   What you mean actually is that they are better than you, that you need their condescending favors . . . Listen, this is how the world works: you got money, respectable Jews start coming your way. Reb Eli, a Hasid, took a nice donation from you. All of a sudden, you're one of the chosen and he's not asking where you got it. Murderer, crook, whatever. If you have it, they'll take it—*Ot-shto*! . . .

The Daddy   Don't crawl too high, Soreh, you hear me? Not too high or one day you'll break your neck. *(wags his finger at her)* Don't push yourself . . . Don't push yourself. I'm telling you, you have a house, stay in it, you have bread, eat it. Stop *krikhn* up to where you're not invited . . . Every dog should know his den . . . *(goes away from the table, gestures with his hand)* I'm killing myself over the whole story . . . I am afraid that this will be our downfall . . .

Soreh   *(stops her work, puts arms akimbo) Mansparshoyn*! Don't you dare be ashamed! I've been a *nekeyve*, a whore, and I can say what was is no longer, fisss . . . flown away. You have nothing to be ashamed of. The whole world is no better . . . Everyone should go around with their eyes to the ground. *(goes to him)* And later on when we have money, we'll pack up shop. No more roosters will be scratching themselves around here . . . Who has to know who you used to be . . .

The Daddy   *(thinking)* That would be for the best . . . I could buy up a stable of horses and export them out like Izzy Wagoner . . . Become a *mentsh* . . . Nobody will look at me as if I were a crook . . .

Soreh   *(thinking)* *Akh*, it's a pity about business . . . You'll never make the same kosher cash in horses . . . Here, we see, you know, ruble in hand.

The Daddy   This is already reality.

Soreh   *(goes into a second room, comes out with a tray of dishes, puts them on the table)* And you see, we have a daughter, *got tsu danken*, a wonderful girl. And like all other respectable girls in this city, she's going to get married. Take an honest *mentsh* for her man, and have the most honest babies . . . You see, and what is the matter? *Akh, vos iz der mer?*

The Daddy   *(getting up, to Soreh)* *Yau*, and are you going to be her teacher? *(angry)* Go, let Manke sneak up to her from downstairs . . . Why don't you let her stay over, *do*, in this house?

Soreh   What's your problem? I asked Manke up here once to teach Rivkele how to embroider. She is a young woman, you know; we have to think about her trousseau . . . Where is she supposed to find friends anyway? You don't even let her out on the street . . . *(pause)* Okay, you don't want Manke up here—fine.

The Daddy   *Neyn*, I don't want her up here—do you hear me? *Neyn*, I don't want her in my house. *(looks to the basement)* Nobody from downstairs can come upstairs and be in my house. Do you hear me? Keep them separated—like cats and dogs, like milk and meat, like gentiles and Jews, like kosher and *treyf*—keep them separated. Downstairs *(points to the basement)* is a brothel and upstairs, this is the home of a pure Jewish girl—a *koshere kaleh meydl*—do you hear me? *(pounds his fists on the table)* A Jewish virgin lives here. Here. *Do*. Keep them separated . . . *(hears feet on the stairs)*

Soreh   Whatever, whatever, just stop shouting. *(listening)* *Sha*. People are coming—Reb Eli's here.

She fixes her hair and pulls off her apron. Yankl straightens himself out. Both stand by the door expectantly. Shlomo and Hindl enter, very much at home.

The Daddy   *(to Sore)* Would you look at me and my guests . . . *(to Shlomo)* Here, I don't do business. Downstairs. Everything downstairs . . . *(looks to the basement)* I will come down.

Shlomo   What are you *yogn* about? What? Are we embarrassing you?

The Daddy   *Haklal*, and what have you come here to say?

Shlomo   You're making *dokh, a shtikl simkhe* here, a little party. We have come to say a *mazal tov* . . . my old friends . . . What? No?

Soreh   Look at me and my friends.

The Daddy   From today on, everything that once was is out . . . You have some business, fine, but everything downstairs. *(shows him to the basement)* Here I don't know you, you don't know me—from today on. You can take a drink of whiskey. *(gives them both a glass of whiskey)* Make it quick; it could be that we're expecting a human being.

Shlomo   *(takes the glass of whiskey and speaks derisively to Hindl)* You see, marriage is an incredible thing. You become a real person, no worse than anybody else. You can have a Sefer Torah written. Not like you pimps, "girls and boys." *(to The Daddy)* You see, I've been watching you, and today I got engaged to this animal, *ot (looks at Hindl) ot.* Hey, don't you think she'll make a pretty housewife? You'll see. She'll put on a wig. She'll look like the real article, a rebbetzin *efsher.* A rabbi's wife, this is what I'm thinking.

The Daddy   We must wish you the best. So *khosn- kaleh*, you're engaged. And when, with luck, is the wedding?

Soreh   Would you look at this? Why the hell is he standing around arguing with them for?! *(to herself)* It suits him—*(to Yankl)* with these fucking *oysvorfs!* May God not punish me for saying it. I'm sorry, God. The rebbe's assistant and the scribe could be here at any moment.

Shlomo   When is the wedding, you were saying? When does an old brother like me ever get married? When we get a couple of *nekeyve*-girls, we'll get married and set up a whorehouse of our own. What else can an old buddy like me become? A rabbi? But the *nekeyves* have to be something extra special—fine, hot and frisky. Otherwise it doesn't pay . . .

The Daddy   And what do you want from me, may you live to hear it? . . .

Shlomo   What do I want from you? Only a *tinykayt.* *(looks at Hindl)* It is your *nekeyve, yo?* And that is my bride. She's got a claim against you. *(takes Hindl's little black book from her)* And from today on, you deal with me—starting right now. Today, I only want a *tinykayt.* A tenner against her book. *(hits his hand on the book)* It's good money, good money. *(moves his eyes toward Hindl)* She wants to buy a chapeau.

The Daddy   Everything downstairs. Everything downstairs. When I come down, we'll work out the arrangements. I can do *gor nisht* for you here. I have no business with you here. *Keyn, shum, nisht.*

Shlomo   By me, it's all one downstairs or upstairs. No stranger lives downstairs. No stranger lives upstairs. *Vsyo ravno*, only one devil.

The Daddy   *(angry)* Collect your bag of bones and get out. *Makh plats.*

Do you hear me? We're expecting people.

Soreh   I hope you have a miserable evening. May an angry night fall on your head, your hands and your feet. You came here to shame our celebration . . . *(looks at Hindl with scorn)* Is it worth the aggravation for that *Federinshlatserin* slut?

Hindl   *(to Soreh)* If I'm not good enough to be one of your whores, you can go downstairs yourself.

Shlomo   *(gesturing to Hindl)* Tell her she can send her daughter down. *(to Soreh)* They would make really good business.

The Daddy   *(going over to Shlomo)* Diddle me, do you hear me? *(looks at his wife)* Diddle her, *Pan brat*, we're old friends. But keep my daughter's name out of your mouth, *du herst?* *(taking him)* Mention her name and I'll slit open your bowels. *Du herst?* She doesn't know you and you don't know her.

Shlomo   I will know her. *Nash brat*. We're old friends, practically family.

The Daddy   *(grabbing Shlomo by the neck)* I'm taking out your bowels. Hit me in my face, kick me with your feet, but don't you dare mention my daughter's name. *(they struggle)*

Soreh   *(running toward them)* You're not ruining this for me! Setting himself up to fight with these *oysvorfs*. Here. When a real person could come in at any moment. *O vey iz mir*—the pain is upon me. Yankl, Reb Eli, the scribe. Yankl, Yankl, remember God. *(pulls him away)* What's wrong with you?

They hear heavy steps outside on the stairs. Soreh tears The Daddy away from Shlomo.

Soreh   Yankl, Yankl, Reb Eli's coming, the scribe's coming. This is a disgrace. It's a scandal for everybody.

The Daddy   No, right here, right now. *(goes after Shlomo)*

Reb Eli   *(from offstage)* Excuse me, *soyfer*, here lives the great patron, our *bal-tsdoke*.

Reb Eli looks in the door, sticking in his big head with his pipe.

Reb Eli   What kind of *geruder* is this? By a *bal-tsdoke*, there should be joy and jubilation in the house. You musn't fight. *(pulls his head back out) (offstage)* Excuse me, *soyfer*.

Hearing Reb Eli's voice, The Daddy lets go of Shlomo. Soreh runs to him and gives Shlomo some money that she took out of the sack, pushes Shlomo and Hindl out the door. Just as they are about to leave, Reb Eli and the scribe are about to enter. They quickly move aside and look away from Hindl.

Shlomo   *(to Hindl, as they are leaving)* Look who his friends are now. Wait, wait, he'll become the big *dozor* in this city. Mugwump. *(they leave talking)*

Eli is a short fat little Jew who speaks quickly with ingratiating hand gestures. He has a high opinion of himself and he feels at home.

Eli   Excuse me. Excuse me, *soyfer*. *(aside to Soreh and Yankl)* Make yourself a little more presentable. It's already time. People are coming.

The scribe enters, a tall elderly Jew, his long thin body wrapped in a broad overcoat. His beard is long, white, and sparse. He wears glasses. He is aloof and mysterious.

Mr. Eli   *(pointing to Yankl)* Dos iz der bal-tsdoke.

The Scribe   *(extends his hand to Yankl, looks him over)* Sholem Aleykhem, Yid.

Yankl extends his hand uncertainly. Soreh respectfully moves to his side.

Eli   *(takes a seat at the table and pushes a chair over for the scribe) Zets Aykh, Soyfer. (to Yankl)* Sit. *(the scribe sits, Yankl unsure sits next to Eli, to the scribe) Dos iz der Yid* on whose behalf I had the Sefer Torah written. *(he pours a glass of brandy for the scribe and then for himself)* He has no son to remember him so he wants to please God with a Torah. This is a custom of the people of Yisroel, and a completely beautiful one I might add. We must help him . . . *L'khayim soyfer. (takes the scribe's hand and then Yankl's) L'khayim bal-tsdoke.* Today, you are the master of celebration.

Yankl stretches out his hand at a loss. Eli drinks. Soreh goes to the table and pushes some of her home-made cakes toward Eli. Yankl pulls her by the sleeve and signals her to move away. Eli drinks.

Eli   *Trinkt soyfer.* Drink, patron. You must celebrate today. God has helped you. You had a Torah scroll written, a Sefer Torah. It is a big mitzvah. It is the greatest of good deeds. It's huge.

The Scribe   *(holds the cup in his hand, to Eli about Yankl) Ver iz der Yid?*

Eli   Who is he? What's the difference? A Jew . . . Not a learned one, no—but does everyone have to be a scholar? If a Jew wants to fulfill a commandment, we must accept him. *(to Yankl)* Drink a *lekhayim.* We are celebrating you.

The Scribe   *Vet er nor visn vi zikh mit a Sefer umtsugeyn?*

Eli   What would he be if he didn't know? He is a Jew. What Jew doesn't know the meaning of a Sefer Torah? *(drinks) Lekhayim, Lekhayim.* May God give complete salvation to the Jews.

The Scribe   *(gives his hand to Yankl) L'khayim, bal-tsdoke . . . (admonishing him)*

36

You should know a Sefer Torah is a great thing. The entire world stands upon the Torah. Each Sefer Torah is just like the two stones *Moyshe Rabeynu* brought down from Mount Sinai. Each line written in the Torah is sacred and pure . . . In a house where there is a Torah, God can be found . . . It must be protected from any impurity . . . *Yid, zolst visen az a Sefer Torah . . .*

The Daddy *(frightened, stammering)* Rebbe . . . Rebbe . . . I want to say to the Rebbe the whole truth . . . I want to say . . . I am a sinful human being, Rebbe . . . I am afraid . . .

Reb Eli *(interrupting him, to the scribe)* This Jew is returning to the answers. As it is explicitly written in the Talmud, we must befriend him. And what would he be if he didn't know what a Sefer Torah was? He lives, as a Jew, you know. *(to Yankl)* You must have respect, *derekh erets* for a Sefer-Torah—*groyse derekh erets* just as if you had a great rebbe right here in your home at all times . . . You cannot speak impertinently in a home where there stands a Sefer Torah. You must protect it with modesty. *(speaking to Soreh, looking around her and not at her)* A married Jewish woman cannot uncover her hair in this home. *(Soreh pushes her hair under the wig)* You may not go to the Sefer Torah with naked hands. For this, in this house where there stands a Sefer Torah, no wickedness whatsoever can happen. In return, it will be constant supplier of riches and success. It will protect the human being from all kinds of anger. *(to the scribe)* What, you think he doesn't know this? They are Jews . . . *(Soreh nods her head)*

The Scribe *Reb Yid.* You hear that entire worlds stand upon the Torah. In the Sefer Torah is the entire existence of the Jews. With one word, *kholile*, with one word you can shame the Sefer Torah and it can, *kholile*, cause a gross misfortune to fall upon all Jews. *Rakhmone Letsalen*, may it never happen!

The Daddy *(standing up from the table)* Rebbe, I want to say everything . . . Rebbe. *(goes closer)* I know that you are a holy Jew. I am not worthy, Rebbe, that you should find yourself here . . . under my rafters . . . Rebbe, I am a sinful human being. *(looking at his wife)* She is a sinful human being. We may never touch the Sefer Torah . . .

He goes to Rivkele's room and takes out Rivkele by the hand. She holds in her hand an embroidered cover for the Torah with a star of David from gold thread.

The Daddy *(about Rivkele)* Rebbe, it's for her. Rebbe, she may keep company with a Sefer Torah. She is as kosher as a Sefer Torah. I had it made for her, Rebbe. *(looks at her work)* See, Rebbe, she embroidered a little skirt for the Sefer Torah's benefit. She can be near it, Rebbe. Her hands are clean. I, Rebbe, *(claps his hand on his heart)* I will not touch your Sefer Torah . . . *(to his wife)* She will not touch your Sefer Torah . . . She, Rebbe, *(puts his hand on Rivkele's head)* only she will go near the Torah. I will keep it in her room until she marries. When she goes out of my house, she will take the little Sefer-Torahle with her to her man . . .

Eli *(to The Daddy)* That is to say, you mean, that when you make the wedding for your only daughter—you will give the Sefer Torah as her dowry—what? No?

The Daddy Mr. Eli, When my daughter marries, I will give a lot of money for her dowry and I will say to her *azoy*: You go out of your father's house and forget . . . forget your *tate* . . . forget your *mame* . . . and have kosher children, Jewish children just like every other good Jewish daughter. *Ot*, this is what I will say to her.

Eli That is to say, you want to present the Sefer Torah as a wedding gift to your daughter's *khosn*, what no? *(to the scribe)*

You see, Reb Aaron, there are still Jews in this world. A Jew has a daughter, and what does he do? He has a Sefer Torah written for the benefit of her bridegroom . . . That is beautiful. It is virtuous. I am telling you, Reb Aaron, is that or is that not Jewishness? This is Yiddish . . . oh, *ahk*, oh . . . *(smacks his lips)*

The Daddy   *(brings Rivkele back to her room, closes the door after her)* Rebbe, I may speak clearly to you. We are alone. My wife may hear it. Rebbe, we are sinful people. I know God will punish us. I have one worry. He ought to punish us. He ought to cut off my leg. He ought to cripple me . . . I'll be a beggar. Only not this . . . *(quieter)* Rebbe, if you have a son and he fucks around and is caught by the devil, that would be one thing. But a daughter, Rebbe; if she sins it's as if your mother in her grave has sinned . . . I went inside to the holy *besmedresh* . . . I went over to this Jew *(looks over to Reb Eli)* and I said to him *azoy*: You give me *epes azelkhes* that will keep my home from sin . . . He makes to me: Have a Sefer Torah written and put it inside your home. Rebbe, we . . . in any case, we've given over our souls to the devil . . . It's for her, Rebbe . . . By her, here in her little room, I will put up a Sefer Torah. She must keep company with it . . . We—may not . . .

Eli privately whispers something to the scribe, making various different gestures with his hand, looking at The Daddy. The Daddy and Soreh stand by the table and wait. Pause.

The Scribe   *(after a short discussion)* And where are the neighbors, the *balebatim*? Who is here to honor the Torah? *Koved—hatoyre?*

Eli   We'll go into to the *besmedresh* where they're all learning. We'll gather up a minyan of Jews. There will already be Jews there to honor the Torah. *(goes to the table, fills up the glasses and slaps The Daddy on the back).* *Nu*—so, God will help. They will celebrate you, patron. God is close to those who master the answers . . . *nishkoshe*, you will give away your only daughter to a Talmud *khokhem*. You'll take a poor yeshiva boy for your son-in-law and you'll give him a living. He will sit and learn the holy Torah the whole day. And on the merit of this Torah, God will forgive you . . . *(pauses)* Listen, I have already inquired about this and actually have my eye on a *khosn*—a rarity, a fine head . . . His father is a very respected Jew . . . *(coughing)* Do you want to give your only daughter a large dowry?

The Daddy   Rebbe—she'll take everything away from me. My *kapote*—take off me . . . Everything . . . Everything . . . And I'll say to her *azoy*: you do not know your *tate* . . . You do not know your *mame*. I will send them around the back. I'll say to her husband *azoy*: You will have your food, your drink, and learn there with your holy Hebrew books . . . I don't know you . . . You don't know me . . .

Eli   Everything will be all right already. On the merit of the holy Torah . . . Come, *soyfer* . . . come, benefactor *bal-tsdoke*—to the *besmedresh* we go. We're looking for a minyan of Jews. We will celebrate this holy book . . . *(to the scribe)* You see, Reb Aaron. A Jew. Although he sins, nevertheless a Jew . . . He has a Jewish soul. He is looking for a Talmud student for a son in law . . . *(to The Daddy)* Nishkoshe, nishkoshe. God will help you . . . God loves the penitent, those who have mastered the answers. Only you must give generously to the Talmud students. You can't do it alone. You must support a yeshiva boy. *Varum al Torah olam omed*—for the world stands upon the Torah . . . *(to the scribe)* Isn't that reality—Reb Aaron? *Nisht vor?* *(to The Daddy)* I knew your father once . . . He was a truly honest Jew . . . was a wagon driver . . . a truly beautiful Jew. Believe me, God will help, and this Jew will live to become like other Jews . . . *(To The Daddy)* Only the point is, you must return to the law completely, that is to say, you can't be going along the same path that you've been on . . . and you must support the Talmud students . . .

The Daddy *(summoning his courage to Reb Eli)* Only let me get together a little more cash, Mr Eli. I just need a little more time so that I can give my daughter a nice dowry or my name isn't Yankl Shapshovitch. Mr. Eli, if I can't do business in my little "shop" here . . . I'll handle horses, I'll handle . . . Like my *tate olev hasholem* . . . I'll put together a stable for the Lithuanian market, and my son-in-law will be here meanwhile sitting and learning Torah. And when I come home for Shabbes, I will sit in a corner and listen to my son-in-law study the lines in the Talmud. Or my name isn't Yankl Shapsovitsh if I'm telling a lie!

Eli *Nishkoshe, nishkoshe.* God will help you. God will help you. *Nisht vor*, Reb Aaron?

The Scribe Who can know? Our God is a god of mercy and compassion but he also is a god of vengeance and retribution. *(starts to leave) Nu*, it has already become late, let us go inside to the *besmedresh. (goes off)*

The Daddy What does the Rebbe mean?

Eli *Nishkoshe, nishkoshe*, God will help you . . . He must help you . . . Come, come, *bal-tsdoke*, take home the Sefer Torah with jubilation and joy. *(about to leave. Yankl hesitates, undecided. Eli notices)* What, you want to say something to your missus— that she should prepare for the coming of the Sefer Torah?

Soreh *(to Eli)* It's prepared, Mr, Eli. Prepared.

Eli *Nu*—so, why are you waiting? The scribe has already gone.

The Daddy *(stands by the door, not sure, pointing to himself)* I can walk together with the Rebbe out on the street?

Eli   Come on, come on, if God can forgive you, then we *avade* can forgive you.

The Daddy   *(enthusiastically)* Mr. Eli, you would be a good rebbe. *(about to embrace Eli then remembers himself and pulls back)* A good rebbe—I should live like that. *(they leave together)*

Soreh is left alone onstage.

Soreh   *(cleaning the room and setting the table, calls to Rivkele)* Rivkele, Rivkele, come inside and help me. They will be here soon with the Sefer Torah.

Rivkele   *(looking in from the door, uncertain)* Isn't he, *Tate*, still here?

Soreh   No, Rivkele. He went to the *besmedresh* with Mr. Eli and the scribe to get the other householders. The head rabbi, the *rov*, will be coming.

Rivkele   *(showing her cover for the Torah)* See how pretty I embroidered it?

Soreh   *(preoccupied)* I see, I see, comb your hair, get dressed, the householders will be coming you know, *Der Rov . . .*

Rivkele: I will go call Manke up. She will comb my hair, I love it so much when she combs my hair. She brushes my hair really pretty and straight . . . Her hands are so cool . . . *(takes something and taps the floor with it calling)* Manke, Manke!

Soreh   *(frightened)* What are you doing, Rivkele? No, your *tate* will scream. It's not appropriate for you to do that. You cannot be friendly with Manke. You are already a young lady, a *kaleh*, about to be married. You come from a respectable home. People are talking about possible matches for you, excellent *shidukhs* with little scholars . . .

Rivkele I love Manke so much.

Soreh It is a disgrace for you to be friends with Manke . . . You are a respectable child, you will be friends with other such children . . . We're talking about possible *khosns* for you. Your *tate* has gone out to see a young man for you. Mr. Eli said so. *(goes into the next room)* We've got to get dressed, wash ourselves clean, the guests will be here any minute . . .

Rivkele A *khosn*? A man for me? What kind of *khosn, Mameshi*?

Soreh *(from the second room)* A little golden *khosn*, a fine young scholar from a really nice family.

Manke appears in doorway and playfully beckons to Rivkele. Rivkele goes over to her, walking cautiously backward, beckoning to her as she does so. The room is quickly becoming dark.

Rivkele *(in Manke's arms—to her mother)* Will he be a handsome *khosn, Mameshi*?

Manke kisses her passionately.

Soreh *(from the other room)* *Yau, tokhtershi*, a handsome *khosn*, with two black *peyes* around his ears with a satin coat and a little velvet *kasketl*—like a rabbi would wear. He is a rabbi's son actually, Mr. Eli said so.

Rivkele *(in Manke's arms stroking her cheeks)* Where will he stay, *mameshi*?

Soreh *(from the other room)* He will stay in your room where the Sefer Torah will be. He will live there with you and learn the holy Torah.

Rivkele *(in Manke's arms)* Will he love me, *mameshi*?

43

Soreh *(as earlier)* Very much, *tokhtershi*, very much. You will have honest children, kosher children.

**CURTAIN FALLS SLOWLY
AS THEY SPEAK**

ACT TWO

In a large basement apartment in an old building, directly below The Daddy's home. Hindl comes in, waits a minute on the step, looking at Shlomo. She is wrapped in a light shawl, made up like a tart in a short dress, inappropriate for her age. She walks around the apartment, stamping her feet with the intention of awakening Shlomo.

Shlomo   *(waking up, looking around)* Is that you? Why aren't you on the street?

Hindl   It started to rain.

Shlomo   *(sitting up on the couch, sarcastically)* O, did you answer me, princess? Have you forgiven me already?

Hindl   I'm not angry anymore.

Shlomo   *Azoy* . . . well if you want you can stay angry. *(lies back down)*

Hindl   *(looks away, runs to a curtain and listens; runs to Shlomo)* Shloyme, I'm not leaving. See, now, we are alone, no one can hear us, tell me, as sure as there is a *got af der velt*, tell me, are you going to bring me to the *khupe*? Are you going to marry me?

Shlomo   *Yau*, princess, shove your savings between your saggy tits and go cry to The Daddy that I took away all your money. *(mocking her)* You don't have anything, not even enough to buy a little hat . . .

Hindl   *Yau*, I said—it made me sick, cut under my heart. You rip the shirt off my back and then go *krikhn* up to that *super-oxide* bitch . . . I'll douse her head in gasoline. How can you

45

stand that stench? She'll put anything in her mouth. What a piece of ass you got there—a real bargain.

Shlomo   You finished? Is this a performance? I'll nail you so hard between the eyes, you'll be looking at your old dead *bobe*!

Hindl   Hit me, cut scars into my body . . . *(pulls up one sleeve and shows him)* you've already marked me blue. *(pulls up the other sleeve)* Please, cut me, pinch me, but only you must say to me here in this room, just as you pray kaddish for your father in his grave, will you really, *af dem rektn emes,* marry me?

Shlomo   *(lying down)* I wanted to once, but now I don't want to.

Hindl   You don't have to want to. I like it like that. Only don't make a fool out of me. You want money, tell me, you want a *kapote*—it's yours. What kind of games are you playing with me, Shloyme? *(moves away from him)*

Shlomo   *Nishkoshe* sweetie, there are plenty of weddings in this world—you'll catch your trout.

Hindl   *(pulling aside the curtain to her bedroom)* What the hell do you care what I do?

Shlomo   Fine. You don't want me to give a shit, I won't. *(pause)* So, are you going to bring me a tea at least? . . .

Hindl brings him a glass from her kitchen, puts it on the table. She goes by herself to her room, starts looking through her clothes.

Hindl   *(after a short pause, from her room)* So, you like her *nu . . . nu . . .* won't you be busy now. Buying handkerchiefs to stuff your wifey's shirt, a pair of stilts to make her human sized, and you'll have to pay a dentist to make her some teeth and yes don't forget the organ grinder—you've got the monkey.

Better get a good hurdy-gurdy barrel organ man to distract the crowds when you cart her around from house to house. I promise I'll throw you a couple of pennies when you start caterwauling by my window.

Shlomo Hold your snout, woman, I'm telling you . . .

Hindl And if I not, what are you going to do to me?

Shlomo *Onpatshn*— *(raises his hand to hit her)*

Hindl *Patshie, patshie, kikelekh.* No, no we don't hit. Today if you hit a woman, she'll come back and stab you with a knife.

Shlomo *(on his feet)* Who'll do that exactly, huh? *(Hindl goes into her bedroom)* Who'll do that exactly? *(she nimbly hides something beneath her clothes)* What do you got there? What the hell are you hiding in that blouse?

Hindl What is going on with you?

Shlomo Show it. I'm telling you. *(struggles with her and pulls out a red blouse; he goes out of her bedroom)* Let's see what we have here. *(he violently tears the blouse; a photograph falls out of it)* Oh, Moisheh the locksmith, so he's been tinkering with your chastity belt. So he must be the rich man. Since when have you been doing him?

Hindl What are you going on about?

Shlomo Oh, what am I going on about . . . *(he hits her; she falls to the bed and cries)* So you've been fooling around with Moisheleh. Photographs were exchanged, a bridegroom couple and I didn't know anything. *(pause, goes to the table)* And I didn't know anything. *(drinks again, puts down the glass, goes up to the steps by the door)* And I didn't know anything . . . *(he stands there by the* *door)* Hindl, come here! *(she doesn't answer)* Hindl! *(stamps his foot and runs furiously off the steps)* Here, I said, do you hear me?

Hindl starts to get up from her bed and move toward him, covers her face with a handkerchief.

Hindl   What do you want?

Shlomo   Did you speak with Manke?

Hindl   *(whimpering) Yau.*

Shlomo   *Nu,* what did she say?

Hindl   *(still whimpering)* That when we have our own little housey she will come over to us.

Shlomo   For sure?

Hindl   *(wiping her eyes)* Yes. She's not coming alone, she's bringing a friend.

Shlomo   For sure, we can't make a living from one whore, we have to pay rent.

Hindl   We would need a fresh one . . .

Shlomo   I know. That would add to our kitty. Where are we getting her from?

Hindl   I have my eye on one *nekeyve*, green as a tree. Still a girl . . .

Shlomo   *(interested)* Can we make a living off her?

Hindl   But she is still . . .

48

Shlomo A girl . . . a *nekeyve* from another house?

Hindl No, a respectable daughter, she still lives with her parents.

Shlomo From where do you know her?

Hindl She comes to Manke every night, sneaks away from her daddy . . . No one sees her . . . She is drawn here . . . She is still so young . . .

Rivkele *(sticks her head in the window from the street, winks to Hindl)* Psst. Is my *tate* here?

Hindl *(winks back)* No.

Rivkele moves away from the window.

Shlomo *(making eyes at Hindl)* Her? The Daddy's daughter? What a kitty, a goldmine.

Hindl *Sha shtil*, she's coming.

Rivkele *(tall and thin, modestly dressed, wrapped in a black shawl; she sneaks in quietly, her heart pounding, speaking more with her hands than with her mouth)* Where's Manke? There . . . *(looking at a closed door)* There with?

Hindl winks yes. Rivkele goes to Manke's door and listens intently, passionately, all the while heart pounding, looking around.

Shlomo *(quietly to Hindl)* Tomorrow we have to go look at the place on Pivneh Street.

Hindl When are you going to bring me to the *khupe*?

Shlomo First we need a place of our own, *dokh*.

Hindl   I wonder who'd know how much the *Rov* will charge for *meseder kidushn zayn,* for doing the ceremony?

Shlomo   We've got to have enough left over to buy furniture – it's got to look snazzy. *(the door bangs open, The Daddy enters)*

The Daddy   *(His face still retains the wildness of his youth. His dress is now respectable. He shakes the rain from his hat.)* How can we make any living in this *regngor? (suddenly spies Rivkele, furious)* What? Here? *(grabs her by the collar and shakes her, gritting his teeth)* What are you doing here?

Rivkele   My mom . . . *mameshi* sent me . . . called me . . . *(crying)* *Tate,* don't *shlog* me.

The Daddy   Your mother, your mother sent you . . . Here . . . *(screaming) Mameshi! (brings her by the collar to the steps)* She brings you here to all this evil. It pulls her . . . She wants the daughter to be what the mother was . . .

Rivkele   *(crying) Tate,* don't *shlog* me . . .

The Daddy   I will teach you to obey your *tate. (drags her out of the room; Rivkele is heard crying offstage)*

Shlomo   Yankele, the gambler's son, doesn't suit to have a whore for a daughter . . . *(from upstairs a loud commotion, a man's heavy steps and a woman's protests)* Does he have to destroy the leather over his wife? Snap. Crackle. Pop. Oy vey . . . oy vey . . .

Hindl   Good for him. A mother should watch her daughter . . . What you were, you were but when you get married and have a kid—watch her . . . You'll see, *az got vet helfen* and we have children, I'll know how to bring them up. In my house, a daughter will be as pure as a *tsadeykes,* a saint with cheeks like rosy beets . . . No eye will fall on her. Marriage—yes. We'll throw an enormous party—a smorgasbord with food from all over the world, and lots a liquor, a sit-down dinner and hundreds of guests and the most famous, most expensive, most popular rebbe will preside. She'll take a strapping young *khosn*, brilliant, beautiful, upstanding, rich. *Khupe ve-kidushin*—it'll be a real wedding . . .

Shlomo   *(slapping her between her shoulderblades)* Listen, baby, if we live, we'll see it. But you've got to speak with Rivkele. Work her, honey, cause brother, without her you can forget about your *khupe ve-kidushin*.

Hindl   Don't worry about it. I'll take care of it.

Shlomo   We'll see. *(pause, quiet)* When you pack her, bring her straight over to me, you know already . . .

The Daddy   *(comes in angrily) Akh.* It's night time. It's *regning.* No dog will be sniffing around here tonight. *(looking at Shlomo)* Enough with the wedding planning. Say goodnight to your *khosn, kaleh. (goes to the stairs and calls) Rayzl, shlof. Basha, shlof.*

From outside are girls' voices, "Coming, coming!" Hindl winks at Shlomo from behind The Daddy, gestures for him to go. Shlomo goes to the stairs, stops on the top step, and looks at The Daddy.

The Daddy   Move, move, it's closing time, enough with the scheming already.

Shlomo   *(shoves his hand in his pockets, looks straight at The Daddy)* Since when did you become such a holy roller?

The Daddy   Wander, wander, I'll tell you another time.

Shlomo   *A ruekh in zayn tatn's tatn's tate arayn . . .*

Hindl	*(runs to Shlomo on the stairs)* Shlomo, go home, do you hear me? Home, I'm telling you!
Shlomo	*(about Hindl)* My bitch . . . *(exits looking at The Daddy)*
The Daddy	Like I need him here . . . *(referring to Hindl)* You can take that rotting carrion with you and set up your little shop.
Hindl	You can't set up shop with a "rotting carrion." Nobody'll pay for an old bitch . . . but with *yunge lyalkelekh*, with young baby dolls.
The Daddy	*(calling in the corridor)* Rayzl! Basha!

Two girls run in laughing, dripping wet. The Daddy exits, slamming the door.

Basha	*(a provincial girl, chubby with red cheeks, naive, speaks with a country accent)* How the rain smells . . . *(shaking off the rain)* Exactly like the apples by us, at my house, left to drain in the garret . . . It is, you know, the first May rain . . .
Hindl	Loopheads to stand in the rain. They want to take in the whole world . . . not even a brain-dead *yold* would show up in this weather . . . *(goes to her room where the curtain is drawn aside, packing)*
Rayzl	*(shaking herself off)* I need them like the spook of a black year. I paid up my little book yesterday . . . We stood under the awning, the rain smelled so tasty . . . it washed the entire winter off my head . . . I wanted to swallow all of it *(goes to Hindl)* See . . . *(shows Hindl her wet hair)* how fresh it is . . . sniff it . . .
Basha	At our house there, at home, at my house, they must be making the first *shtav*, cold soup with lots of fresh vegetables, I know, when the first May rain comes, when it pours, the May rain, in our house they've already cooked *shtav*

and borscht. I love them . . . And the goats must be already grazing in the fields. And rafts must be already swimming on the water . . . And Franek takes the *shikses* to the bar and dances with them . . . And all the wifeys have to start baking cheesecake cause it's almost *Shvues* . . . You have to have cheesecake on *Shvues*, *avade*. *(pause)* Do you know what? I am going to buy a new summer *pelerine* and go home to visit for this *Shvues* . . .

She runs into her room and comes back with a big summer straw hat that she begins arranging in the mirror.

Basha You see how I'd look on *Shvues* strolling down to the *kolye* in this *kapelush* . . . *Akh*, they'd *plats*, they'd poop out their bile from envy. What, no? I would go but I am scared to death of my father . . .

Rayzl What, he'd hit you?

Basha He'd kill me on the spot. He's been looking around for me with an iron pipe. He once found me with Franek dancing at the *kretshme* and he gave me such a clap on my hand with a pipe. *Ot*, *(she shows them her hand)* I still have a scar to this day. *(pause)* I came from a good home—my father is a butcher. The guys that I could have married, the *shidukhs* I could have had. *(speaks in a lowered voice)* One *shidukh* I could have had was with Notke, the meat cleaver. I still have the gold ring he gave me. *(shows the ring on her hand)* He gave it to me *kholemoyd sukes*. Oy, he wanted to become my *khosn*, only I didn't wanna.

Rayzl Why didn't you wanna?

Basha Because I didn't wanna . . . He stinks of ox flesh . . . Brr . . . They called him Shtinky. Go marry Shtinky and every year make another little Shtinky . . . Brr . . .

Rayzl And what do you have here . . .

Basha Here I am, you know, a free woman. I have my basket of fancy underpants, respectable outfits, dresses at least a little bit prettier than any rich man's wife back home. *(she brings a dress out from her room)* If I wore this down Marshalkovske Street, I'd become a sensation . . . tsss, sparks would fly. *Akh*, I wish everyone I knew in my town could see me in this dress. *(throws it around her)* I'd sashay down from the train station. They'd explode out of spite . . . In a fit of poopooplexy, right there and then. They'd drop to the ground, writhing in agony on the sidewalks. *(she saunters around in the dress)*

Rayzl *(fixing her dress and hat)* *Ot azoy*, put your head a little higher. Who needs to know that you were ever in such a house? You will say that you work in a business. A count fell in love with you . . .

Hindl *(from her room)* And what is the matter with this house? We are not, *efsher*, just like any woman in business? Today the whole world is like this. The modern world desires it. Today even respectable daughters are no better than you. This is our job, not our life. And when one of you gets married, like me, you'll know what your man needs. Unlike some woman in a shop, we know the value of a man . . .

Basha *(walking around the apartment fills in the pause)* Yeah, right. Like they wouldn't already know. The heart tells. My mother died because of it. She couldn't bear it. I've never even been to her grave. *(stops suddenly)* Sometimes she comes to me at night in a dream. I see her. She comes to me in her burial shroud and she brings me some *shtav* to eat. And then when I go to take it her hands turn into prickly thorns and she grabs my head and starts ripping my hair out by the handful . . .

Rayzl *Mame-kroyn!*—your own mother! Did you see her? What did she look like? A dead mother. Was she pale . . .

Hindl Shut up. Where do come up with this crap? Tales from the crypt. Listen, the dead aren't going to come in here: our *balebos* put a Sefer Torah upstairs to protect us all . . . *(thinks for a moment)* Didn't his wife, our *baleboste*, work in a whorehouse for as much as fifteen years and then get married? Is she not a decent little wife? . . . Hasn't she kept all the commandments that a *Yidishe tokhter* is supposed to keep? . . . Isn't *efsher*, Rivkele, her daughter, a kosher, pure child? And our *balebos*, isn't he an honest man? Has he cheated any of you? He is creating the most beautiful, most important object in Jewish law—*di sheynste nedove*, a Sefer Torah, he is paying a man thousands to handwrite the Bible, to recopy every blessed word from God—is there anything more honorable than that? . . . *a Sefer Torah gelozt shraybn* . . .

Rayzl People are saying that you should never read a Sefer Torah that has been commissioned by such a man. And a daughter with a mother like that will never be anything better than a whore . . . I am just quoting what they're saying. They long for it, the *yeytser hore*, they carry the evil inclination in their blood. It drags them toward the *shmut*. That's what she said to me.

Hindl *(frightened)* Who said that?

Rayzl An old *bobe, a kishef makherin* told it to me . . . It's just like witchcraft . . .

Hindl It is a big fat lie . . . Who is she, the witch? I'll scratch out her eyeball . . . as sure as there is a *got af der velt* . . . We have a great God in this world . . .

Manke slinks out from under the curtain of her little room, half naked. She has thrown on a light shawl. We can see her high, colored panty hose, her mussed

55

hair. She is very supple and has a long, boldly beautiful countenance. She is still young; a lock of her hair falls across her forehead. When she speaks, her eyes dance, then suddenly a shiver goes through her entire body, and we have the feeling that her bones would break all together. She looks around, surprised.

Manke   What? Nobody's here?

Rayzl   *(seeing Manke, tidying up)* Manke, is that you? Good, I'm glad that you're here. *(looking at Hindl)* She was about to make me into a rebbetzin. Where did you leave your *yold*?

Manke   He fell asleep. I snuck away.

Rayzl   A real prince, maybe. Did he buy you a beer?

Manke   Ah, he was a nutty little guy from Lithuania. Third time coming to me. He's always bugging me: "Who's your daddy? Who's your mommy?" like he wants to make a *shidukh* with me . . . He kisses, he hides his face in my breasts, closes his eyes and smiles like a babe full of milk. *(looks around)* Rivkele isn't here yet?

Hindl   *(laughing pleasurably) Geven* . . . She bumped into The Daddy . . . He made a ruckus.

Manke   Oh, shit . . . When?

Hindl   A while ago . . . He fell asleep already, of course. *(quietly)* She'll come back down soon, of course.

Rayzl   *(excitedly to Manke) Kum*, Manke, we're gonna go stand on the street. It's *regning* outside, drops like pearls . . . The first May shower. Who's gonna go outside with me and stand in the rain?

Manke   *(goes to the window)* It's raining outside. What a gentle rain.

Mmm, and how it smells . . . *Kum* . . .

Basha   By us, at home, when it pours rain like that, the *rinshtokes* overflowed and flooded the tiny little streets and we'd go around barefoot and dance in the rain . . . Who's taking off their shoes? *(takes her shoes and socks off to dance)* Take off your shoes, Manke, we will go dance under the rain . . .

Manke   *(takes off her shoes and socks, loosens her hair)* The rain will soak us from head to toe . . . You grow taller, you know, if you stand under a May rain. Right, Rayzl?

Basha   *(running) Kum*, we'll pour water all over one another . . . Let's sprinkle each other with handfuls of *regndrops*. *(loosens her hair)* Let's drench ourselves, raising our arms as if we were trees . . . *Kum.*

Hindl   Wait, wait. The Daddy is not asleep yet. He'll still hear us.

All listen with their ears to the ceiling.

Rayzl   Get outta here, can't you hear him snoring? . . .

Manke   Wait, let's knock for Rivkele in the quiet.

Basha and Rayzl go off. Manke taps softly in a corner of the ceiling for Rivkele. From outside, we hear the girls jumping around in the water.

Girls   *(taking handfuls of water and throwing it through the open door of the house)* Come out! Come out!

Rivkele   *(sticks her head out the window. She is wearing a nightdress, with a light shawl wrapped around her. Softly)* Manke, Manke, did you call me?

Rivkele   Manke, Manke, did you call me?

Manke	*(takes a chair, puts it under the window, crawls up, taking Rivkele's hand)* Yes. Rivkele, I called you . . . *Kum*, we will stand under the May rain, we will splash each other with water—it'll make us grow taller . . .
Rivkele	*(from under the window)* Shush, speak more quietly, I snuck out of my bed . . . So *Tate* can't hear me . . . I am scared; he must not *shlog* me . . .
Manke	Don't be afraid of your father, he won't hop out of bed so quickly . . . *Kum*, it'll be better to stand under the rain. I am going to let loose your hair. *(Runs her hands through Rivkele's long black hair. From under the window)* *Ot azoy*, I will wash your hair in the rain.
Rivkele	I am only in my nightdress . . . A whole night I laid in bed waiting for my *tate* to fall asleep so I could sneak out to you. I heard your knock and I slipped out of bed . . . So quietly I snuck out barefooted, so *tate* wouldn't hear me.
Manke	*(takes her passionately)* *Kum*, Rivkele, I will wash your eyes in the rainwater, the night is so likable, the rain is so warm, and everything smells just like the air . . . *kum* . . .
Rivkele	Shut up . . . Shut up . . . I am scared of my *tate* . . . He *shloged* me . . . He locked my room . . . and hid the key in the Sefer Torah . . . I laid there a whole night . . . I heard you calling me . . . You called me *azoi shtil* . . . I snuck out the key from the holy cabinet without making a sound . . . My heart was pounding so hard . . . pounding so hard . . .
Manke	Wait, Rivkele . . . Wait . . . *Ot*, I'm going to you . . . *(jumps up from the chair, leaves the cellar)* I'm coming to you . . . I'm coming to you.

Manke exits. Rivkele disappears from the window. Hindl, who has been

listening to the conversation between Manke and Rivkele with great atten-
tion by the curtain of her room speculating, now walks noisily up and down,
thinking out loud, talking to herself slowly.

Hindl It's a sign from God, I'll pack them both, Rivkele and Manke, and take them today, tonight . . . I'll bring them there
to Shlomo . . . Here, here's your bread with butter . . . Rent
an apartment, put up a *khupe*, become a human being no
worse than anybody else . . . Call the rebbe and poof I've
arrived (*stops abruptly in the middle of the room, ruminating, raises her*
hand to the ceiling) Our father in heaven, you are a father to all
orphans . . . Mommy in your grave, intercede for me . . . Let
me go to the edge! To a purpose! . . . (*pause*) If God grants me
this, I'll commission a Sefer Torah in His honor for the shul
. . . And every *shabbes*, I'll bring three pounds of candles to
the *besmedresh* (*a long pause; she is lost in the fantasy of her fortune*)
He is a good God . . . A good God . . . Father in heaven . . .
Mommy, Mommy, speak for me . . . Don't be silent . . . Intercede for me . . . Tear down worlds . . . (*goes to her room and*
begins to gather together her things from her room and packs them into her
basket) Let me only first of all be ready . . .

Hindl goes behind her curtain. A long pause. Manke enters, bringing in
Rivkele, cuddling. They are both wrapped up in the one wet shawl. Their hair
is dripping wet. Large drops of water fall from their clothes to the floor. They
are barefoot. Hindl, standing behind her curtain, listens.

Manke (*speaking with a restrained passion and love; softly but with deep resonance*)
Are you cold, Rivkele? Cuddle with me . . . Good to cuddle
you in me. . . Warm yourself in me, so good to have you in me
. . . Come on, we will sit down here, both of us, on the divan
(*brings her to the divan, sits down with her*) *Azoy, azoy* . . . Put your
face in my breasts . . . Yes . . . *Azoy* . . . Caress me with your
body . . . So cool, like the water running between us . . . (*pauses*)
I uncovered your breasts and washed them in rain water that
ran in my hands . . . Your breasts are so soft and smooth . . .

59

And the blood in them cools under my hand, like fresh snow . . . like frozen water . . . they smell like meadow grass . . . I let down your hair . . . Just like that . . . *(runs her fingers through Rivkele's hair)* I held you and washed your hair under the rain; see, it smells like the rain. *(she buries her face in Rivkele's hair)* Your hair smells of the May rain, so light, so soft . . . and so fresh . . . like meadow grass . . . like an apple just picked off a tree . . . Cool me with your hair *ot azoi. (she washes her face with her hair)* Make me shiver . . . but wait . . . I want to comb out your hair like a girl bride . . . a part with two long black braids. *(combs her hair)* Do you want to, Rivkele? Yes, do you want to?

Rivkele   *(nodding her head)* Yes, yes.

Manke   You will be the *kaleh* . . . A beautiful bride . . . It's Friday night, you're sitting with Mamashi and Tatashi around the table . . . I—the *khosn* man . . . Come to visit you . . . Do you want to, Rivkele? *Yau, du vilst?*

Rivkele   *(nodding her head) Yau, ikh vil.*

Manke   Wait, wait . . . Your parents have gone to sleep . . . The *khosn-kaleh* meet at the table, we're shy . . . Do you want to?

Rivkele   *(nodding her head) Yau,* Manke.

Manke   Then we go slowly toward one another: you are my *Kaleh,* I your *Khosn* . . . I take you in my arms, *(takes her)* I hold you tight and we kiss each other very softly, quietly, *ot azoy. (kisses her)* We kiss each other . . . Our cheeks turn red, we're so bashful . . . It is good Rivkele, *gut?*

Rivkele   *Yau,* Manke . . . *Yau* . . .

Manke   *(lowers her voice, whispering in her ear)* And then we lie down and sleep in one bed, nobody sees us, nobody knows, only you and I just like that. *(presses her to her)* Do you want to sleep with me through the night, *azoy*, in one bed, *vilstu?*

Rivkele   *(caressing her all over)* Ikh vil . . . Ikh vil . . .

Manke   *(drawing her to her)* Kum . . . Kum . . .

Rivkele   *(quietly)* I am afraid of my *tate* . . . He will wake up . . .

Manke   Wait, Rivkele, wait . . . *(caresses her for a moment)* Do you want to go with me away from here? We will be together the whole day, the whole night . . . Your father will not be there, your mother will not be there . . . Nobody will scream at you . . . Nobody will *shlog* you . . . We will be alone . . . the whole day . . . It will be so much fun, *vilstu*, Rivkele, do you want to?

Rivkele   *(closing her eyes)* My *tate* will not know?

Manke   No, we will run away at once now at night with Hindl and go into her home . . . She has a home with Shlomo, she told me, you will see, how good it will be . . . A lot of young people will come, officers . . . We will be alone the whole day . . . We will dress up like soldiers and ride around on horses. Come, Rivkele, do you want to? *Yau, vilstu?*

Rivkele   *(with a pounding heart)* My *tate* won't hear us?

Manke   No, *neyn*, he will not hear, he sleeps like a bear. *Ot*, you hear how he snores . . . *(runs to Hindl's room, grabs her by the hand)* Do you have place? Come quickly, take us away! . . .

Hindl   *(eager)* Yes, yes, quickly to Shlomo. *(she grabs a dress, throws it on Rivkele)* He will take us there at once.

Manke   *(quickly dressing Rivkele)* You will see how good it will be . . . How much fun it will be.

She dresses Rivkele, everyone grabs what they can by hand, a shawl, a coat.

61

They slowly walk up the stairs. They meet Rayzl and Basha, who are coming back into the room. Basha and Rayzl look at the women in surprise.

Rayzl and Basha   Where you going?

Hindl   Don't make a sound, not even a peep, we're going for some beer, lemonade . . .

Hindl, Manke, Rivke off. Rayzl and Basha look at each other shocked.

Rayzl   I don't like that story.

Basha   Me neither.

Rayzl   There's something going on—oh, shit . . .

Basha   *(looks at her in terror)* What is it?

Rayzl   Look, it has nothing to do with us. We will put off the light and go to sleep. We don't know from nothing. *(extinguishes the lamp; each girl goes to her room in the half dark)*

Rayzl   *(going off)* She spoke it right—the card turner. Oy, she spoke reality . . .

For a second no one is seen onstage. Dark. Then Basha runs wildly out of her room, half undressed, with a hysterical cry.

Rayzl   *(moving the curtain from her room)* What's with you, Basha?

Basha   I am spooked to lie down. I imagine my dead mother with her prickles and her thorns coming at me, twirling around in my room.

Rayzl   The *Sefer Torah iz posl gevorn*—we have been defiled— O, nothing to protect us now.

Basha	I'm scared that now it will not be a good night. My heart shivers inside of me.

A commotion is heard from above, a scraping of furniture. The girls listen, terrified. Soon a noise is heard of something heavy falling down the steps.

The Daddy	*(shouting)* Rivkele, Rivkele, Where are you?
Rayzl	*(to Basha)* We will lie down to sleep. We don't know from nothing. *(both of them lie down and pretend to be in a deep sleep)*
The Daddy	*(running around with a light in his hand, hair disheveled, a coat over his night clothes, shouting wildly)* Rivkele, Rivkele is here? *(nobody answers; he throws back the curtains to the rooms)* Rivkele, where is she? *(wakes up the sleeping girls)* Where is Rivkele! Rivkele, where is she?
Rayzl and Basha	*(rubbing their eyes)* What? We don't know nothing.
The Daddy	You don't know . . . You don't know?

Runs quickly out. He can be heard bounding up the stairs. Then silence. A noise is heard of something dashing down the steps. The door bursts open noisily. The Daddy tumbles in pulling Soreh by the hair. Both are wearing nightclothes.

The Daddy	*(Drags Soreh to the floor by her hair. He points to the brothel.)* Your daughter, where is she? Your daughter?

Basha and Rayzl both stand pressed against the wall, petrified.

QUICK CURTAIN

ACT THREE

Room as in the first act. The cupboard and bureau are out of place. Pieces of laundry, clothes are strewn all over the floor. The door to Rivkele's room is open, the light from a candle in her room comes across the stage. Soreh, with messy hair, with a dress untidily thrown on, goes about the house, picking up the thrown things, putting them in a bag as if preparing to leave, but she eventually puts most things back where they belong. Gray early morning. The gray light of day comes through the windows.

Soreh *(collecting the things)* Yankl, what's doing with you, Yankl? *(goes to the open door in Rivkele's room and looks in)* Why are you sitting? *(turns back and continues picking up things)* A misfortune . . . time is running out! The whole house he wants to overturn . . . *(goes again to the door)* Yankl, why are you shutting upping? What is doing with you? *(turns back in tears)* A man sits by the Sefer Torah and broods and broods—what is there to brood about? A misfortune—it happens, go to the police, get the commissioner . . . Find that youth by any means necessary— legal or otherwise. There is still time left . . . *(returns to the door)* Vos shvagstu? Vos shvagstu? *(she sits down on a bag by the door, puts her face in her hand and starts crying)* Like a *meshugener*, he sits there all alone, stares at the Sefer Torah, *mermeling* something with his lips . . . *Ani*—he doesn't even hear me. *Ani*—he doesn't even see me. Why is he doing that with himself? *(gets up to The Daddy at the door).* It makes no difference to me. You want me to go away—I am going. The devil's not going to take me. I'll make my own bread. *(returns to packing, silently, pause)*

The Daddy *(Comes out of the room without his hat or coat, his hair a mess. His eyes look wild. He speaks slowly in a quiet, hoarse tone.)* I will go . . . You will go . . . Rivkele will go . . . Everything will go . . . *(points with his finger to the cellar)* Everything into the whorehouse . . . God

65

doesn't want it . . .

Soreh   Yankl, why are you doing that with yourself! You've become crazy . . . *(goes to him)* Reason what you're doing. An accident happened—what man escapes misfortune? Come, we're going to find Shlomo. We'll give him 200, 300 rubles. He must give us our baby back . . . That kid'll do it . . . Why are you sitting? Why are you doing that with yourself?

The Daddy   *(in the same voice, wandering around the room)* It's all the same pile of vomit to me . . . I gave over my soul to the devil . . . Nothing will help . . . God doesn't want it . . . *(he stands by the window and looks through the lattice of the shutter)*

Soreh   God doesn't want it . . . Deluding yourself, you don't want it . . . Do you love your child? Yankl, Yankl, *(pulling him away)* what has become of you? Reason, while there's still time . . . Meanwhile, he could be carting her around the country while we wait here. Come over to that youth . . . That bitch brought him to her, obviously. Why are you standing? *(abruptly)* I sent for Eli. We will hear what he has to say. *(pause; The Daddy looks through the window)* What are you looking at? *(pause)* Why don't you answer me? Oh, *Mameh-kroyn*, someone's going to go crazy. *(turns away from him and starts crying)*

The Daddy   *(as earlier, going around the room)* No more house . . . No more wife . . . No more daughter . . . Into the brothel . . . Back to the brothel . . . We don't need a daughter . . . We don't need her . . . whores, like her mother became . . . God doesn't want her . . . Back to the housey, into the whorehouse . . .

Soreh   You want into the housey? What's this? Pay back time—my *kapore*. What a business I've got. *(returns to her packing)* He wants to destroy this house . . . What's doing with him? *(thinks a moment)* While you lie there catatonic, I'll take over. *(takes off her diamond earrings)* I'll go around to Shlomo. I'll give him my diamond earrings. *(she looks in the bag and takes out a gold chain)* I'll give him this gold chain, and if he holds back, I'll put down another hundred. *(she searches Yankl's pants pockets for money; he doesn't stop her)* Rivkele will be here in less than fifteen minutes. *(she grabs a shawl as she leaves)* He'll do it for me. *(slams the door after her)*

The Daddy *(wanders around the room alone, his head down)* *Say vi say*, it's all one to me . . . The devil has taken over . . . No more daughter . . . No more Torah . . . Everything into the housey . . . Into the housey. . . God doesn't want it . . .

Long pause. Reyzl looks in the door, sticks in her head. Sneaks into the room and stands near the entrance. Yankl notices her and stares.

Reyzl *(stammering)* I went after Mr. Eli . . . The missus sent me . . . He's coming right now . . .

The Daddy *(looking at her for a while)* *Say vi say*, the devil has taken over . . . God doesn't want it . . .

Reyzl She was such a respectable girl . . . It's such a shame, *nebekh* . . .

The Daddy looks at her in wonder.

Reyzl *(apologizing)* The missus told me to wait here until she came back.

The Daddy Don't be afraid, I haven't gone crazy yet . . . Not yet . . . God punished me . . .

Reyzl Who could have guessed such a thing would happen . . . She was such a good little girl . . . What a shame, *nebekh* . . . In all my life, I never . . .

Eli *(coming in with a lamp)* What's happened? Why call me all the way here so early in the morning? *(looks through the shutters)* We should be davening already . . .

The Daddy *(not looking at Eli)* The Sefer Torah has been violated. Reb Eli, fatally defiled.

Eli *(frightened)* What are you saying, *Yid? Kholile!* The Sefer Torah? What's happened? What have you released on the earth? The entire city will have to fast . . .

The Daddy Even worse, Reb Eli.

Eli *(agitated)* What are you saying? The entire city could be, God forbid, involved . . . What has happened? Tell me, *Yid. Reboynu shel oylem!*

The Daddy Down to the whorehouse . . . below with them . . . *(points to the floor and then to Rayzl)* Into the whorehouse . . . No more Torah . . .

Eli *Yid,* what are you talking about? What did you do with it? *Zog!*

Reyzl *(at the door, calming Eli)* No, Rebbe, not the Torah, the daughter . . . Rivkele. The Sefer Torah is kosher. *(points to Rivkele's room)* It's in there . . .

Eli *(breathing a sigh of relief) Gloybt hashem yisbarekh.* But is the Sefer Torah kosher?

Reyzl *Yau,* rebbe.

Eli *(calm, spitting out) Geloybt hashem yisbarekh*—I was killed with the fright . . . *(to The Daddy)* Why were you speaking foolishness? *(to Reyzl without looking at her) Avek* . . . Is she still not here? *(to The Daddy)* Has anybody gone looking for her?

The Daddy By *mir*, my daughter is holier than a Sefer Torah.

Eli Stop blathering *narishkaytn* . . . Just shut up. *Shvayg*. Stop making a hullabaloo. Has anyone gone looking for her? To bring her back? What do I know? Why are you standing here?

Reyzl The missus has already gone after her.

Eli Do we know where she's gone?

Reyzl *Yau*, the missus will bring her home any moment.

Eli *Dokh*, that's good. *Vos-zshe*, why were you screaming . . . The whole world will have heard about it before long. You have to keep these things *shtil* . . . It's not pretty . . . If your future in-law becomes aware of this, it'll cost a couple hundred more . . .

The Daddy *Say vi say*, it's all one to me . . . Everybody could know. I don't care. I have no daughter . . . I have no Sefer Torah . . . Into the whorehouse—everything goes to the whorehouse . . .

Eli Eh, have you lost your mind . . . It was an unfortunate occurrence . . . Unfortunate things happen to people. God should protect us . . . What? When? God helps . . . Everything will remain intact. *Der iker*, the important thing is that nobody knows . . . You didn't hear it, you didn't see it. Wipe your mouth and make like you know nothing . . . *(to Reyzl)* It should not *kholile*, go any further . . . *gehert? (turns to Yankl who is staring into space)* I saw the . . .

He looks around to see if Reyzl is still there. Seeing her, he stops. After a pause, he begins again, more softly looking at Reyzl as a hint for her to leave.

Eli I had a talk with . . . with . . . *(looks at Rayzl again; she finally leaves)* I met with the bridegroom's father at the *besmedresh* between *minkhe* and *ma'ariv*. I spoke with him. The Jew is amenable to the situation. I even let him know, *derekh hagav*, that the bride isn't from the greatest *yikhus*. Modern times people don't even look at such things . . . *Meyle* anyhoo, for another hundred . . . *Avade* on Shabbes, God willing, I'll sort things out with the Jew . . . We will go together to the rebbe to test the *khosn* . . . Only the important thing is here, *der iker* is that nobody should know, nobody should find out about this little incident, *Kholile* . . . It could do damage . . . The Jew has *yikhus*—the *khosn* has a good head . . . *Nu, nu,* calm yourself. Take God's help and everything will go smoothly . . . Now with God's help, I am going home to get myself ready for davening. When the little girl shows up, let me know immediately . . . You hear me? *(as he is leaving)* Right away, for God's sake—*lemen hashem* . . . *(about to leave)*

The Daddy   *(gets up and grabs Eli's arm)* Listen, sir, you take your Sefer Torah with you. I don't need it any more . . .

Eli   *(thunderstruck)* What are you talking about? What do you want? Have you become crazy? Are you insane?

The Daddy   My daughter has gone into a brothel . . . The Sefer Torah is defiled . . . God punished me . . .

Eli   *(trying to interrupt him)* What are you talking about?

The Daddy   I am a sinful man. I know it so well . . . He should have broken off my foot, buried my head . . . a young death . . . From my child, what did he want? From my poor child?

Eli   You listen to me. You may not talk like that against God.

The Daddy   *(agitated)* You may say everything . . . The truth . . . I am *take* Yankl Shapshovitsh, a pimp, The Daddy of a whorehouse.

You may even speak the truth to God . . . I am not afraid any more . . . I went to you in the *besmedresh* . . . I told you everything . . . You told me to have a Sefer Torah written. It's in there. I put it in her room. All night long I stood outside her door and I spoke to God. I said: If you really are a god . . . you know from everything, everything I do . . . You will punish me . . . Punish me . . . Punish my wife . . . We have sinned. But my innocent child—on my poor child have mercy . . .

Eli Nothing bad has happened to her. She will come back . . . She will become a real Jewish housewife yet—*a gants yidish vaybl* . . .

The Daddy *Say vi say* . . . The devil has taken her . . . He'll draw her in . . . She's already made her start . . . She won't be able to stop . . . If not today, tomorrow . . . Her soul has been delivered to the devil . . . I know this . . . O, I know this.

Eli Stop speaking foolishness . . . Be still . . . Beseech God for forgiveness in your heart . . . Overcome your livelihood . . . Your daughter will, with God's help, get married like all other Jewish girls, and you will be proud of her yet . . .

The Daddy *Farfaln, Rebbe, oy farfaln* . . . If only she had died young, Rebbe, I wouldn't have said anything . . . If she died, I would know that I had buried a kosher Jewish child . . . I would go to her among the graves of our fathers and say to myself *azoy: Ot*, here lies your child . . . *you* are a sinful man, here lies yours, a kosher child, an honest child. But so, what have I become in this world? I say to myself: *you* are a sinner . . . left behind a generation of sinners . . . After you . . . and so the sin continues from generation to generation, *fun dor tsu dor* . . .

Eli Would you stop speaking like that? A Jew does not speak like that. You asked God for help and say to him it's hope-less?! *Farfaln!?*

The Daddy *(interrupting him)* Rebbe, please don't persuade me . . . I know that it is already hopeless . . . The sin lies on me and on my house, like a noose around my neck . . . God didn't want me . . . Only I ask you, Rebbe—Why didn't God want me? Why didn't he bother to save me, Yankl Shapshovitsh, from the swamp that sucks me down? *(goes in to Rivkele's room and gets the Torah, holds it up and speaks)* You, Sefer Torah! I know you are a great God! You are our God . . . I, Yankl Shapshovitsh, have sinned . . . *(claps his fist to his heart)* My sin . . . My sin . . . Make me a miracle, send down a fire that rages, and I'll stand in it! You open up the earth and swallow me in it . . . Only take care of my child . . . Return her to me as pure and as innocent as she once was . . . I know that for you anything is possible . . . Do a miracle . . . You are a great God . . . If you don't . . . You are no God . . . I'm telling you, I, Yankl Shapshovitsh, am telling you that you are no God . . . You are vengeful, like a man you are . . .

Eli *(jumps up and grabs the Torah from Yankl)* Do you know to whom you are speaking? *(looks at him and goes into Rivkele's room)* Beg the Torah for forgiveness!

The Daddy You may tell even God the truth to his face. *(follows Eli into the room)* If he is a God, he should show us his miracle here in this place . . .

Reb Eli and The Daddy go offstage. Soreh runs in.

Soreh *(runs in excitedly; begins fixing her hair and dress by the mirror) Kum*, come in, Shlomo. Why are you standing there behind the door?

Shlomo *(by the door)* Where is Yankl? He should know *(comes in)* for a *nash brat* I would do anything, even though he has hurt me.

Soreh   *(runs to Rivkele's door, locks Eli and Yankl inside)* Leave him to rest, *(smiles)* he's become a real religious fanatic recently—a *fru-mak* . . . Hangs around with the *frume yidn. (runs over to the main door and locks it)* Collecting *kaleh*-brides, are we? What an annoying bitch Hindl is—you'll never get rid of her, *dokh*. She follows you around like you are already hers . . . She'll arrive here any minute, huffing and puffing, *avade*, looking for you . . . *(smiling)* O, Shlomo, O Shlomo— acquiring wares? *(she goes over to the window and opens the shutters; the room grows lighter)* Why have they shut the place up? It's like a funeral in here . . .

Shlomo   Don't worry about it, I told you. I told you yes once already. Yes is yes. I wouldn't do this for anybody—for you I will do it, although recently you've been treating me very badly . . . Well, forget about it . . . Hindl can work it out in her own head—for all it'll help her . . .

Soreh   *(goes over to him, grabs his hand, and looks in his eyes)* You are so young, do you need to take a *moyd* like her? Who is she? Dragging her fallen ass around from brothel to brothel. As young as you are . . . You could now grab a small fortune, you need her? A young man with a few hundred bucks lining his drawers. Can't you take a decent girl? Why not? I'm asking you, aren't you as young as any other? *(slaps him across the shoulders)* Talk to me, Shlomo. You know, I wasn't too bad to you once . . . Even though I've neglected you lately, *dokh*, I was always the same Soreh. Say something, why not? *(looks into his eyes)*

Shlomo   *(twirling his moustache)* Ah fuck . . . The devil knows why I let that woman twist my head . . . It was only temporary . . . Until I could get together some cash—a couple of groschen

. . . You don't think I really meant to marry her. My mother would have cursed every vein in my body . . . I have a respectable mother, you know . . . And my sister?!

Soreh   Have you no other business prospects than to have your head twisted by such a slut? Are you really going to set up a whorehouse with her? What do we have now, I mean really, from all the houses? It doesn't pay to hang around with *oysvarfs . . . Oysvarfs. (goes to him and gives him her earrings)* You take those for yourself. Here, take another hundred and tell me where Rivkele is.

Shlomo   What is reality? This is reality . . . You were once a good Jewish woman—*a gute yidene. (winks at her)* Lately, you've been spoiled. But when it comes down to it . . . you should know that Shlomo is your *nash brat . . . (takes the earrings and puts them in his pocket)*

Soreh   Tell me where she is, Shlomo, now . . . You can tell me everything even though I am her mother . . . You know I am not frightened by such things . . . Tell me, have you brought her away somewhere . . . to a . . .

Shlomo   She is very close by . . . Like I told you, I will bring her to you, I will bring her . . . Do you hear me? What a year it's been on me already. What a whore she could have been. *Ir blik, ir shik . . .* She's fucking gorgeous. She's elegant. You've really screwed me here, bitch. You *mamzered* me . . .

Soreh   Ha, Soreh can still . . . Tell me, Shlomo, where do you have her? You can tell me everything. . . *(takes him by one hand and slaps him on the other shoulder playfully looking into his eyes) Yau . . .* tell, good brother!

Shlomo   Not far from here . . . not far . . .

A thumping of fists is heard on the outside door.

Hindl *(off)* You don't know from her . . . You don't know from her . . .

Soreh Let her knock her head on the wall . . . Look how she clutches him in her paws . . . *Kha . . . Kha . . .* He cannot even leave her for a second . . . *(making eyes at him)* You should be ashamed of yourself, carrying on with older women . . . *(Shlomo thinks a moment; Soreh grabs his arm and pulls him aside)* Talk to me . . . Why do you need her? I will get you a girl . . . You will see. *(winks at him)*

Hindl *(breaking the door open, running in)* What are they in a rage at him for? . . . They've suffered through a miserable night, their daughter ran away . . . *(grabs Shlomo by the hand)* You don't know where she is. What do they want from you?

Soreh *(sits down on a chair, looks at Shlomo suggestively, and then points to Hindl)* There she is—your she-beast. *Kha. Kha, kha . . .*

Hindl *(looking around)* What an evil laugh she has . . . *(to Shlomo)* You don't know anything about her. *(pulls him aside, quietly)* We're going to go far outside this city to Lodz . . . There, we can put up a *khupe* and get married . . . Rent an apartment . . . our two *nekeyves*, remember, what are you doing? You don't know from her . . . *(pulling him out)* *Kum*, Shlomo . . . *(he is undecided)*

Soreh *(loudly with a pleasing smile)* *Nu*—so, why don't you go with her, Shlomo? She came after you . . . Go away to another city to Lodz . . . put up a *khupe* . . . rent an apartment . . . tee-hee. *(goes closer to Shlomo and draws him away from Hindl)* Such a young man like you with a respectable Jewish *mame*, a religious *tate* . . . What does she want from you? Why is she picking at you?

Shlomo *(calling)* Come on, Soreh, let's go get Rivkele.

Hindl *(putting her hand over his mouth)* You will not tell . . . You don't know from her. *(runs in front of the broken door)* I won't let you leave. *(goes to Shlomo, grabs him by the hand)* Remember, Shlomo . . . they're allowed to and we're not?! Come on, Shloyme, we're getting out of here . . . What a living . . . What a life we could make together . . .

Shlomo We've heard it already . . . We've heard it . . . *(pushes away from her)* Listen, we'll talk later. I don't have time right now. *(goes out with Soreh)*

Soreh *(runs back, unlocks Rivkele's door, and calls out)* Rivkele is here!

Hindl *(in the corridor)* I won't let you . . . You will not tell . . .

Shlomo *(at the door)* Come on, Soreh.

Soreh *(running after Shlomo)* I'm coming, Shlomo.   *(Shlomo, Soreh, and Hindl exit)*

Eli *(comes out with Yankl)* Gloybt tsu got! Gloybt tsu got! *(following Yankl who is pacing around the room)* And you see now how *hashem yisborekh* helped you, *ot* . . . He punishes, *take*, but he sends the antidote before the plague . . . Even though you have sinned, even though you blasphemed his name . . . *(admonishing him)* From now on, you must take it upon yourself never, never to speak those words again . . . You must have respect—*groys derekh erets* . . . You should know what a Sefer Torah is, you should know what a Jew a *lamdn* is . . . You must go to the *besmedresh* . . . Give a huge donation to the yeshiva . . . And fast a *tanis* so that God will forgive you . . . *(pause; sternly looks at Yankl, who continues to pace, absorbed in his thoughts)* Vos, you don't hear me? With *hashem yisborekh's* help everything will go through smoothly. I am about to go to the *khosn's* father . . . We'll shmooze through the details . . . Only you should not haggle—a hundred more, a hundred less. You should know who he is and who you are . . . Have the dowry ready up front and don't sit there *balamutshen* about the wedding . . . God forbid, that we're faced with another disaster, *kholile*. We cannot delay any longer . . . *(looks at Yankl) Vos*, you don't hear me? I'm speaking, you know, to you!

The Daddy   *(to himself)* One thing I want to ask her, *nor eyn zakh* . . . She must tell me the truth. The whole truth. *Yau oder neyn.*

Eli   Do not sin! Thank God for all he has done for you.

The Daddy   *(as earlier)* I will do nothing to her . . . I only want the truth: yes or no.

Eli   The truth . . . The truth . . . God will help . . . Everything will go through smoothly . . . I am going now to speak to your future in law. He is in the *besmedresh* waiting for me. *(looks around)* Tell your missus to tidy up the place . . . And you get the contract in order . . . He must have no time to become aware of the realities of the situation and withdraw . . . Set a date for the wedding and send your *kaleh* away to the *khosn's* family . . . Only don't *balamutshet. Sha shtil.* No one should become aware of the reality . . . *(ready to go)* And you empty out your head of this foolishness. Take God's help and be clean . . . His father mustn't, *kholile*, suspect anything . . . *(at the door)* And tell your missus to make this place decent. *(exit)*

The Daddy   *(pacing as earlier around the room)* Only she must tell me the truth . . . the pure truth. *(long pause)*

Soreh   *(at the door)* Come inside, *kum*, your *tate* will not *shlog* you . . . *(pause)* Get inside, I tell you.

She pushes Rivkele in. Rivkele has a shawl over her head. She stands silent, not moving, at the door, a defiant look in her eyes, biting her lip.

Soreh Why are you standing there, my daughter, my life? You've made us proud for our labor . . . for our effort . . . We'll reckon with you later. *(interrupting herself)* Go inside . . . Comb yourself, put on a dress. A man needs to come . . . *(to Yankl)* I met Reb Eli; he has gone after the young man's father . . . *(looks around the place)* A *khurbn* after me—this place has been ravaged. And look what you look like. *(she begins hastily tiding up)* O, you look like shit!

The Daddy *(staring at Rivkele, goes to her, takes her gently by the hand, and brings her to the table)* Don't be afraid, I will not *shlog* you . . . *(he sits)* Sit here beside me. *(moves a chair near her)* *Zets zikh.*

Rivkele *(angry, hides her face in the shawl)* I can stand also.

The Daddy Sit down. *(he seats her)* Don't be afraid.

Rivkele *(from behind the shawl)* Why should I be afraid?

The Daddy *(faltering)* Rivkele, tell me, Rivkele . . . You are my daughter, I am your father. *(looks at Soreh)* That is your mother . . . Tell me, *tokhter*, the whole truth tell me . . . Don't be afraid of me . . . Don't be ashamed in front of me . . . It's not about your sin, not your sin. It's about mine, about mine, about your mother's sin . . . Our sin . . . *Zog mir, tokhter.*

Soreh Give a look how he sits her down for a cross examination . . . What does he want from her? She's barely alive! Let her go in get dressed. A man needs to come soon, you know. *(goes toward them to take Rivkele from her father)*

The Daddy I'm warning you, leave her alone. *(pushes Soreh away from Rivkele)*

Soreh He's gone crazy today, *meshughe*, what's doing with him? *(goes back to cleaning)*

The Daddy *(sitting Rivkele beside him)* I am not going to hit you . . . *(puts his fingers around her slender throat)* If only I had twisted your neck *ot azoy* before you grew up, it would have been easier for you and easier for me . . . Don't be afraid, I will do nothing to you . . . God didn't punish us for your sin. For ours. I took care of you like the eye in my own head. I had a Sefer Torah written for you, for your life . . . I put it in your room and begged God all day and all night: protect my child from evil . . . Punish me, punish your mother, but take care of my child . . . When you grow up, I will make the best *shidukh* for you . . . I will get you a decent young man for a *khosn* . . . I will keep you both here and pay for everything . . . You will both live . . .

Rivkele *(from under the shawl)* I still have time to get married . . . I am not so old.

Soreh Quite the contrary, my dear . . .

Rivkele They want to make me into a rabbi's wife. Why was my mother not married earlier?

Soreh Shut your snout before I slap it out of you! Figured it out. One night out and she's figured it out.

Rivkele *(not understanding) Yau,* I know already . . .

The Daddy Leave her alone! *(quickly)* I only want to ask her one thing . . . The truth tell me . . . I will not *shlog* you. I will not even touch you, you are not guilty . . . *(cannot get out the words)* Speak openly to me, *dos . . . dos . . . dos . . .* whole truth *zog mir . . . dem emes . . .*

Soreh What kind of truth should she tell you? What do you want from her?

The Daddy	I'm not asking you. *(arises, takes Rivkele by the hand)* Don't be ashamed in front of me . . . I am a father, I am . . . You can tell me everything . . . Speak openly . . . Are you still . . . are you still as pure as when you left here? Are you still a kosher, Jewish child?
Soreh	*(pulls Rivkele from Yankl's grasp)* What do you want from her? The child doesn't know about *shlekhts.* Leave her alone.
The Daddy	*(holds Rivkele tightly in his hand, tries to look in her face)* You tell me the truth, I will believe you . . . Look me in the face . . . straight in my face . . . Are you still a kosher Jewish girl? Look me in the face, straight in my face!

Rivkele, despite his efforts, manages to hide her face in the shawl.

Soreh	Why don't you take that *tukh* off your head? A *tukh* in the house? *(Soreh pulls it off; Rivkele hides her face in her dress)*
The Daddy	*(screaming)* You tell me now, *yezt* . . . Don't be ashamed . . . I will do nothing to you. *(holds her tightly by the arm and tries to look in her eyes)* Are you still a virgin? Tell me here in this place.
Rivkele	*(tries to hide her face in the dress)* I don't know . . .
The Daddy	*(screaming)* You don't know . . . You don't know, then who does know? . . . What do you mean you don't know? . . . Tell me the truth . . . *Zog,* are you still a . . .
Rivkele	*(pulling herself away from her father)* And it was okay for my mother to do it? And it was okay for my father to do it? . . . I know from everything already . . . *(hiding her face in her hands)* *Shlog* me, hit me!

Soreh runs over to Rivkele ready to hit her. Yankl casts Soreh aside with a single blow. She falls into a chair huffing and puffing. Rivkele falls to the ground and starts crying hysterically. A long pause. Soreh, upset, paces the room. Eventually she begins to sweep. She then goes over to Rivkele, lifts her by the hand, and leads her offstage into the room. Yankl does not move.

Soreh   *(runs over to Yankl, takes his hand, and begs)* Yankl, think about what you are doing, remember God, who needs to know about it? *(pause)* Just relax . . . *(pause)* Rivkele will get married; we will still be proud of her life. *(The Daddy is silent)* Put on your *kapote*, they'll be here any moment. *(looks at The Daddy abruptly)* Who needs to know about it?

The Daddy is silent, focusing on one spot. Soreh brings in Yankl's coat and puts his hat on him. The Daddy lets her dress him.

Soreh   It was so unfortunate . . . Such a stupid thing to have happened. Go make yourself right . . . *(straightens Yankl's coat, runs into Rivkele's room; she is heard hiding something there and returns)* We'll deal with you later. *(finishes straightening the house)* Children these days, *oy-oy* . . .

Steps are heard on the stairs.

Soreh   *(running to The Daddy, pulls his sleeve)* They're coming, remember God . . . Yankl . . . Everything can still turn out good . . . *(Reb Eli enters with a strange Jew)*

Soreh   *(pushes her hair under the wig, stands in the door ready to greet the guests)*

Eli   *Gut Morgn.*

Soreh   *Gut Morgn—gut yor.* Welcome, *borekh habo.* *(a little confused, she places chairs before the guests and motions them to sit)*

Eli   *(cheerfully)* Where is the bride's father, *der mekhutn?* *(looks around for Yankl)*

Soreh	*(with a smile, bringing Yankl over to the guests)* Yankl, come make an appearance, please. *(she moves a chair closer to Yankl; everyone says Sholom Aleichem and they sit)*
Eli	*(gesturing with his hand)* Let's get right to it. *(to the stranger, pointing to Yankl)* This Jew wants to make a *shidukh* with you. He has a kosher Jewish virgin and he wants to give her a *talmud-khokhem* for a husband. He'll support the two of them to the end of their days.
The stranger	*Mhikhi Tisi*, that sounds inviting.
The Daddy	*Yau, Reb Yid*, a kosher Jewish virgin . . . a kosher . . .
Eli	*(to the stranger)* He'll give you five hundred right now to sign the contract. Room and board . . . for the rest of their lives . . . He will treat your son like his own child.
The Stranger	*Meyle*, well, I don't need to boast about my wares. In another two years . . . he sits two years and studies—he has the proof in his pocket.
Eli	That we know. This Jew here will take care of him like the eye in his own head. He will have here everything that is good. He'll be able to sit and learn *tog un nakht*.
The Daddy	*(looking at Rivkeleh's room)* *Yau*, there, he will sit and learn in the holy Torah. I have a kosher Jewish daughter. *(goes into Rivkeleh's room and pulls her out by the hand; she is half dressed, her hair is a mess)* *(looking at Rivkeleh)* A kosher Jewish virgin. She will marry your son . . . have kosher, Jewish children . . . like any other Jewish daughter . . . *(to Soreh)* *Vos?* No? *(laughs wildly at the stranger)* *Yau, yau, mekhutn*, a kosher Jewish wifey to be . . . On her wedding day, my own wife will lead her under the *khupe* . . . Into the whorehouse! Downstairs! *(pointing to the cellar)* Into the whorehouse! *(drags Rivkeleh by her hair to the door)*

Get down into the whorehouse!

Soreh   *(running wildly) Gevald! Mentshn!* He's gone mad! *(she tries to get Rivkele away; he pushes her aside and drags Rivkele out by the hair)*

The Daddy   Into the whorehouse down . . . *(goes out with Rivkele; her crying can be heard from offstage)*

The Stranger   *(shocked and terrified) Vos iz dos?*

Reb Eli beckons to him, pulls him by the sleeve, and points to the door. The stranger stands motionless in astonishment. Reb Eli draws him to the door. They leave. Pause.

The Daddy   *(comes back with Eli, whom he meets on the stairs)* Take the Sefer Torah with you. I don't need it anymore.

CURTAIN

GLOSSARY

Yiddish	English
azoy	so
af dem rektn emes	swear to God
onpatshn	hit
a ruakh in zayn tatn's tatn's tate arayn	may a spirit enter your father's father's father
a Sefer toyrah gelozt shraybn	a bible should be written
avade	of course
az got vet helfn	if God will help
bal-tsdoke	big donor
balamutshen	to babble on
balebos	boss
baleboste	mistress of the house
besmedresh	house of study
bobe	granny
di sheynste nadove	the most beautiful donation
dokh	you know
efsher	maybe
geven	was
got af der velt	God in this world
hashem yisborekh	Blessed be the name of God
kholemoyd Sukkos	days between the Jewish holiday of Succoth
ikh vil	I want to
kaddish	prayer for the dead
kaleh	bride
kapelush	hat
kapote	coat
kha	ha (phlegmy laughter)
khokhem	genius
kholile	God forbid

khupe	wedding canopy
khupe v'kidushn	wedding canopy and blessing
khosn	groom
kishef-makherin	witch
kolye	store
kum	come
krikhn	crawling
kretshme	inn
lamdn	scholar
Mame-kroin	Mother dear
Mameshi	Mommy
meseder kidushn zayn	giving the wedding blessing
moyd	girl
neyn	no
nekeyve	whore
nishkoshe	don't worry about it
nu	so
ot, ot azoi	oh, like this
oy	oh
oy vay	oh my
patshie, patshie, kikelekh . . .	patty cake, patty cake . . .
platz	burst
polcrina	slip
rebbe	rabbi
rebbetsin	rabbi's wife
regn	rain
regngor	downpour
rinshtakes	gutters
rov	rabbi
Sefer Torah (Seyfer Toyre)	books of the Hebrew bible

Sefer toyrah iz pasol gevorn	the Bible has been defiled
Shabbes	Sabbath
Shavous	Jewish holiday
shidukhs	marriage matches
shikses	non-Jewish girls
shlog	beat
shtav	a cold soup
shtil	quietly
shul	synagogue
superoxide	peroxide
tate	father
tsadeykis	female saint
vilstu	You want to
yold	idiot
yau	yes (rhymes with paw)
Yidishe tokhter	Jewish daughter
yetser hore	evil inclination
yungeh lyalkelekh	young dolls

MOTKE THIEF

INTRODUCTION TO *MOTKE THIEF*

Motke Thief has a distinguished New York history, beginning over a century ago. The most popular Yiddish daily, the *Forward*, wrote of the original production starring David Kessler in 1917 that "there were moments that one forgot he was in a theater." Critic Moshe Nadir wrote of the same production: "How frightening! How deep! How terrific!" Isaac Samberg played the title role to sold-out crowds in Europe, and the impresario Maurice Schwartz, who acted with Kessler in the original, directed *Motke Thief* for his Yiddish Art Theater in 1922, starring Muni Wiesenfriend as Motke (Wiesenfriend, "the finest young actor of his generation," later became the Academy Award winner Paul Muni).

In this three-act epic drama with a prologue, Asch depicts a society in transition at the dawn of a new century. Religion gives way to secularism, and capitalism conquers all. Just as Puzo and Coppola did decades later, Asch portrays the rise of an underworld dynasty by capturing the outlaw destiny of a charismatic antihero. A psychological portrait of a criminal, the play begins with Motke's poverty-stricken childhood, his education by thieves, and his burning desire to make his mother proud. At the close of the play, when Motke is betrayed by his fiancée and her family, a ruthless criminal is born, never to turn back, and any hope for redemption is gone for good. Asch's Jewish underworld is the ghetto's ghetto, and his fictional Motke foreshadows the very real crimes of Bugsy Siegel, Lepke Buchalter, Meyer Lansky, and Murder, Inc.

In *Motke Thief*, however, Asch writes about more than just criminal life; he attempts a larger view of early twentieth-century society. He creates not one world but four—the poverty of a small courtyard community in Eastern Europe, the world of a traveling low-rent circus, the inner life of a Warsaw café frequented by the Jewish underworld, and the home of the comparatively respectable café owner, whose daughter Motke wants to marry.

Born in Kutno, Poland, in 1880, Asch had been writing plays for over a decade when, in 1917, he decided to adapt his novel *Motke Thief* into a work for the Yiddish stage in New York City, where he was living at the time. As a young man, Asch abandoned his religious studies to become a writer and spent a few years slumming in the Warsaw underworld before moving to NYC's Lower East Side.

Historically, artists and criminals have always lived side by side, poverty and unfettered ambitions bringing them close together. It was this milieu that provided Asch with much of his early inspiration—the dank, dark basement where Motke lives with his drunken father and abused mother, the circus he runs away to, and the seedy café that becomes his base of operations.

Although his work at the time of *Motke Thief*'s premiere was already considered both world class and cutting edge, Sholem Asch had yet to become one of the most controversial Broadway playwrights in American theater history. While his plays were performed in Yiddish and a half-dozen other languages throughout the world, they had not been translated into English. The controversy surrounding his most often translated play, *God of Vengeance*, kept the focus away from his many other excellent dramas.

Despite the illicit settings and roster of hardened criminals in his work, Asch investigates the social conditions that create his characters' deviant reality. He impresses upon us the horrors of Motke's childhood, which cursed the boy from the day he was born. As the play opens, Motke's fate has already been sealed. The twelve-year-old clutching the boots and bread he has stolen for his mother runs through the town, chased by villagers screaming after him: "Thief! *Ganev!*" That same mother, who pleads to the assembled villagers for clemency for her son, says to him once they are alone: "You should have leaked out of your mother's *boikh* [belly] before you came out into the world." Even worse, knowing that their small cellar room is not big enough for both Motke and his father, his mother kicks her son out of their home before he is a teenager.

In fact, even from birth Motke did not have enough food to eat: his mother sold her breast milk to another family. As Reb Meyer, the schoolteacher who shared the cellar room with Motke's family when Motke was still an infant, says: "I once lived with them in the cellar. When the child started to cry, the beams shuddered from his howls. I used to take a stick of sugar wrapped in a rag and give it to him in his mouth, he should think that it was his mother's breast, but he wouldn't let himself be fooled; under no circumstances did he want the little rag."

Routinely beaten by his drunken father, Motke has no real childhood and no education. Later on, in the second act, when Khanele asks him if he would like to read her book, he answers, "I can't read. I never learned." As rough as Motke can be with his other girls, he is tender toward his mother and Khanele his fiancée, as he once was toward Mary the tightrope walker, his first love, until he dumped her for the more respectable girl.

Asch's text reveals a deep understanding of the grifter mentality: a desperate bid to stay alive by playing all sides. In order to escape the circus, Mary, the tightrope walker and prostitute, makes love to both the strongman Kanarik and Motke, causing them to fight. She then wakes up the impresario, Alter Terakh, to stop the fight, robs the john, gives the money to Motke, denies doing it, then confesses she did it but thought Motke was Kanarik. She tells both men to meet her later, then has Motke kill Kanarik and steal his passport. She runs away with Motke to Warsaw and is rewarded with her greatest wish: to become a higher class of prostitute, with clients who can afford to pay for a hotel room.

Asch first wrote *Motke* as a serialized novel in the *Forverts* newspaper in 1916. He was then the most popular Yiddish writer in America. The story of Motke was so beloved that new episodes appeared on the paper's front page. During the same time period, his play *A Shnirl Perl* (*A String of Pearls*) premiered in Philadelphia and later New York, while his one-act *With the Current* opened in English at the Neighborhood Playhouse, a storied theater that also produced works by James Joyce, George Bernard Shaw, and W. B. Yeats.

While the novel *Motke Thief* was set in Warsaw, its leaner stage adaptation, written on New York City's Lower East Side, is infused with an American sensibility unique to the play. In this translation we reintroduce some elements from the novel for their theatrical qualities and the fact that they are too (literally) colorful to leave out. Most of our additions are to the stage directions and scene settings. We take Terakh's costume—red tights and sash, heavy black boots, no shirt, and a chest full of heavy medallions—from the novel. We also include Shlomo's sniggering hunchbacked sidekick, Yona Malpeh, who follows Shlomo around like a dog.

The most significant difference between the play and the novel, however, is that in the novel Motke is arrested, cowering in fear under a table as the police barge in. In the play, however, he escapes out into the world, reflecting an American optimism for a prosperous future, even among the criminal class. With his red velvet suit and his pack of girls, Motke has come so far from the hungry little street urchin he once was, and it is impossible not to want him to succeed. It is easy to imagine the Motke from the play escaping out the window and ending up on a ship to America, on his way to becoming a major gangster here. In the play, Motke reads like a character with a great destiny. At the end of the novel he's more or less finished. Unlike the novel, the play, despite the antihero's many setbacks, ends with a message of hope: Motke's last words to his mother (and indeed the last words of the play) before he jumps out the window and evades the police are "Go on."

Both Yankl, the brothel owner in *god of vengeance*, and his younger, more vicious twentieth-century counterpart Motke underscore the humanity of the criminal, his doomed attempts at reform, and the hypocrisy of the respectable people in society who look down upon such outcasts. The supporting characters in both scripts also entwine the fates of these two antiheroes. Two prostitutes from *god of vengeance*, Basha the naïf and Rayzl the fortuneteller (now called Red), return in *Motke Thief* at the beginning of act two. So does Shlomo, the young pimp who challenged Yankl in *god of vengeance*, although now he is older with a thick red neck and a paunch. Both plays focus on a man who has lived a wild and dangerous life in order to get a financial foothold in society.

What's more, Motke is full of qualities that would decades later become gangster clichés in mob films. He's quick to fight, he sleeps around, and he is so obsessed with his mother that he physically pummels anyone who dares impugn her good name. And through Motke we discover, as with Yankl in *god of vengeance*, that it's impossible to leave the game: once you're in, you're in for life. Like Michael Corleone in *The Godfather*, Motke fools only himself with his dreams of an alternate life in a legitimate business. No one else believes he could possibly lead a respectable life—at least not for long.

Asch knows how to create sprawling and compelling plots. But even more striking is the gritty sexuality and vibrancy of his dialogue. In *Motke Thief* the character of Alter Terakh, the traveling circus impresario and pimp, speaks in a mutated dialect made up of many languages, including German, French, Polish, Spanish, and Russian. In order to create this multilingual character and underline his theatricality for our audience, we translate some of his Yiddish words into French. Given Terakh's involvement in the sex trade, we translate the word *nekhpa*, which can also mean *disease* or *epilepsy*, more pointedly as *syphilis*. The john in act one, a Polish gentleman, or *pahn*, we left with the original Polish moniker but spell it *pawn*, a simple pun in English indicating his role in the scenario.

This translation is not an adaptation: it is a literary translation that stays as closely to the original text as possible. In our work, we look to imitate both Asch's phrasing and diction and to include a layer of the original Yiddish in the translation so as not to sever it sonically from the cultural specificity of the source text.

Yiddish words or phrases appearing in our translations are meant to mark moments of intense or increasing emotion—during the lesbian love scene between Rivkele and Manke in *god of vengeance*, or the passionate conversations between Motke and Mary in *Motke Thief*. We also leave many of the words that deal with marriage and family in Yiddish to underline the implied intimacy of these conversations. If a Yiddish word is used and then followed by its English equivalent, it is because Asch repeats the phrase in his script.

Our translation strategy developed a new layer with *Motke Thief* as it became clear a newer modern world was emerging from Asch's plays that in some ways is symbolic of the shift away from Yiddish among the descendants of Eastern European Jews in America. Although

Motke Thief is set in Poland, Asch wrote it on the Lower East Side while dealing with the fact that his own children were no longer speaking Yiddish.

In a letter to his son Nathan written in New York City in 1917, the year *Motke Thief* premiered in Yiddish, Asch writes: "My dear son Nathan, I wanted to write to you for so long only I didn't know in what language. That is my tragedy that I cannot write to my son in the language that I speak with my people. English I don't know and Yiddish you don't know . . ." Therefore, the Yiddish that we use in this translation also symbolizes an older world, or another world. The café owner and his wife speak a lot of Yiddish at home at the top of the third act. When Der Pawn, a non-Jew, leaves the room, Terakh speaks angrily to Motke in Yiddish. And when Motke wants to write a letter home to his mother, he has it written for him in Yiddish, asking Red if she can write in that most expressive of Jewish languages. Red responds in the affirmative, in a direct translation from Asch: "Yea, my bobe taught me."

It has been long journey to get to this point where we can share this world premiere English-language translation with you today. Many people have supported us along the way. *Motke Thief* was translated with a commission from the National Foundation for Jewish Culture in 2002 with support from the Karma Foundation and was developed through readings by Todo con Nada and the Faux Real Theater Company (Mark Greenfield, artistic director). The prologue for *Motke Thief* was performed for the first time at the Eldridge Street Synagogue in the fall of 2003 (Hanna Griff, program director). The first act was performed at the National Yiddish Book Center (Nora Gerard, program director) in July 2005 and again in August together with the second act of Sholem Asch's *god of vengeance* during the HOWL Festival at the 14th St. Y in conjunction with the Stella Adler Studio (Tom Oppenheim, artistic director).

We also had a great gift from one of the last remaining Yiddish theaters in NYC: Aaron directed a reading in Yiddish of *Motke Ganev* in February 2005 for the Folksbiene (Zalmen Mlotek, executive director) featuring Isaiah Sheffer, Mercedes McAndrew, and Caraid O'Brien, which gave us a deep insight into the original rhythms of the script. And lastly, we were deeply grateful to premiere the play at University Settlement, an organization that played a historic role in assimilating the Yiddish-speaking communities into American life, not least of all by educating them artistically in dance, music, and theater. Kate Guenther, the director of development at University Settlement, was instrumental in bringing us to their stage.

Every culture in America goes through a period of violent entrepreneurship as it attempts to establish itself in society, from the Italian and Jewish mafias of the twentieth century to the Chinese and Latino gangs of today. The fastest and ultimately costliest way to the American dream is through crime—the bootlegger Joe Kennedy becomes the father of an American president. Our Lower East Side staging of Sholem Asch's *Motke Thief* in its English-language world premiere at University Settlement, the first settlement house in America (founded 1886), restored this forgotten tale to the very neighborhood where it was written and where it debuted in Yiddish in 1917, in the very building where many of its original artists and audience were first educated and introduced into American life.

The contributions of Yiddish speakers to American films (Samuel Goldwyn, Paul Muni), theater (Irving Berlin, George and Ira Gershwin), and literature (Henry Roth, Saul Bellow) are extraordinary. With our inaugural production at University Settlement, we strove to reverse the transfer—bringing Yiddish culture to an American audience and its latest generation of immigrants by introducing them to the epic universal tale of a good boy gone bad—*Motke Thief*.

ORIGINAL CAST

Young Motke	Gurjant Singh
One-Eyed Leyb	Mark Greenfield
Zlatke	Laura Barnett
Efraim	Aaron Beall
Berish Miester	Bern Cohen
Dobtshe	Marlene Hamerling
Reb Meyer	Penny Bittone
Blind Perl	Corey Carthew
Shprintse	Ana Da Piedade
Soreh-Rokhl	Leah Emmerich
Velvl	Maureen Sebastian
Izzy	Devin Sanchez
Fruma-Leybtshe	Devin Sanchez
Motke Thief	Jonathan Butler
Terakh	Mark Greenfield
Kanarik	Corey Carthew
Mary	Caraid O'Brien
Der Pawn	Aaron Beall
Reb Meylekh	Bern Cohen
Hindl	Marlene Hamerling
Khanele	Maureen Sebastian
Basha	Leah Emmerich
Girl from Zokhlin	Ana Da Piedade
Rayzl	Devin Sanchez
Shlomo	Penny Bittone
Yona Malpeh	Aaron Beall
Another thug	Mark Greenfield
Customers at Café Varshe	The Company
Policemen	The Company

DRAMATIS PERSONAE

Young Motke	a 12-year-old boy
One-Eyed Leyb	his father
Zlatke	his mother
Efraim	a shop owner
Berish Miester	a smithy
Dobtshe	his wife
Reb Meyer	the *melamed*
"Blind" Perl	a local official
Shprintse	a gossip
The Girls	(Soreh-Rokhl, Fruma-Leybtshe, Velvl, Izzy)
Motke Thief	a young man
Alter Terakh	a circus impresario
Kanarik	a circus strongman
Mary	an acrobat and prostitute
Der Pawn	a Polish gentleman
Reb Meylekh	café owner in the old city of Warsaw
Hindl	his wife
Khanele	his stepdaughter
Basha	a prostitute
The girl from Zokhlin	a prostitute
Rayzl aka Red	a prostitute
Shlomo	a pimp
Yona Malpeh	his hunchbacked sidekick
Other thugs	
Customers at Café Varsheh	
Policemen	

Setting	A Jewish city, circa 1916

PROLOGUE

The stage is set as a poor cellar room. Zlatke is washing clothes. We hear cries outside: A ganev! A thief!
She looks horrified. The door opens and Young Motke runs in out of breath; he is a small boy of 12. He holds
a stolen pair of boots and a loaf of bread under his arm.

Young Motke *(running in terrified)* Mama!

Zlatke *Vey iz mir.* You? Run, your father will come and he will kill you, *do* on the spot.

Motke They're chasing me!

Zlatke What else have you done now? Who is chasing you?

Motke See? *(he holds up the boots)* Hide them, you will have for the winter, I stole them from Efraim.

Zlatke *Aroys fun mayn* house. I don't want you with your stolen goods. *Aroys!*

From outside the cries become nearer: A thief! A ganev!

Motke *(terrified)* Mama!

Zlatke *Vos* should I do with you, unlucky child? They will murder you. Crawl under the bed, get down already, you should have leaked out of your mother's belly before you came out into the world. *(she pushes him under the bed and covers him up)* You will rot in the jails, even to Siberia they will send you.

Efraim *(comes in, without a coat with messy hair)* *Gevald!* Help, he screwed me, in broad daylight, he screwed me. *(shouting)* People! People!

Men and women come in with sticks and brooms.

Soreh-Rokhl He ran in here. I saw him myself, how he ran into the cellar.

Shprintse If he's One-Eyed Leyb's, then you're right. In his mother's *boykh*, he was already a thief.

Efraim He screwed me. He ruined me like an ox is slaughtered—in the middle of a sunny day! *Oy vey iz mir!*

Soreh-Rokhl *(to Zlatke)* Where do you have him?

Fruma-Leybtshe Give up the thief!

The Girls *Ganev!*

Zlatke *(standing in front of the bed)* I have not seen him, I do not know where he is. What do you want from me?

Shprintse *(to the crowd)* What a little maggot! Before he could walk, on all fours, crawling, he was already a thief. You couldn't even let a kid out in the middle of a sunny day, he'd see a child with a bagel, with a roll, *khaped* and devoured. A piece of challah, a little plate of kasha—*khaped* from your hand and *gegobbled*. What he sees, he *khaps*. A little *mamzer*, since we first saw him crawl around on all fours, *a shrek ongefaln af alemen*. You wonder why he is such a thief? His mother taught him.

Efraim Help, my boots, my shoes, he screwed me, he ruined me, in the middle of a sunny day, ruined, people, people! Why are you silent!

Izzy Where is *der yung*?

Fruma-Leybtshe Give out *der yung*!

Zlatke I do not know where *der yung* is, I do not know, I have not seen him, I do not know.

Berish the master craftsman runs in like a wild man—a stocky Jew with bushy eyebrows, thick hair, a hairy face, and a belt in his hand.

Berish Just let me through. Just let me through. Zlatke, give over the boy. It is better for him, I should give him the belt, you will thank me later, Zlatke.

Dobtshe Get out of here, you should work over the kid, for what, they will be grateful? They will curse you even.

Efraim See, see, people, help! *(he finds the boots on the floor)* My blood, my flesh, see how my blood boils, see!

Izzy *(to Zlatke)* Give over the kid, this minute, give over the kid, we're telling you, a robber, he'll grow up to be. *(tries to look under the bed)*

Zlatke *(grabs a nearby stick)* Get out of here! I will not let you do it, I will not let you harm my child. You feed him, that you should beat him? You go near him and I will split open your head.

Shprintse See, people, see, his own mother makes him out for a thief, his own mother.

Berish *(with his belt)* Zlatke, this is for your own good, you should kiss my hand, that I am going to beat him.

Dobtshe   You have the strength for him? He is your child? Will they pay you for it then? You will destroy your health.

"Blind" Perl enters. He is a big man, a local official with a sword.

Reb Meyer   Jews, get out of the way, The Blind Perl is coming!

Efraim   Panya Natsholnik! Panya Polkovnik, our good father, he screwed me, you know, he ruined me, in the middle of a sunny day ruined my little bootsies, my shoes, my blood and my flesh.

Blind Perl   Shh . . . *Posmotrim*, I'll put things in order. *(to Zlatke)* Where have you hidden him? Spill it, chop, chop!

Zlatke   I have not hidden him, I have not seen him, I don't know, what do you want from my life?

Blind Perl   You don't know? *Nu, pasmotrim*, we'll see.

He looks around the room, comes to the bed, tries to look underneath it; Zlatke blocks him.

Blind Perl   Aha! Hey, shithead! *Vilyezi! Vilyezi!*

Zlatke   Dear people, have mercy. *(she blocks his way)* I will not let you touch him, I will not let you. *(wrestling with the official)* He is not guilty, he is still a child.

Blind Perl   A child? So? . . . *(forcefully)* Move away this minute! You won't let me execute the law? . . . Yids, get him out of there.

Berish and Shprintse want to go toward Zlatke.

Zlatke   Your eyes, I will scratch out with my nails, whoever comes near me. *(she starts to cry uncontrollably, then composes herself)* Jews have mercy, have mercy, he is, God forbid, not guilty.

Fruma-Leybtshe He is not guilty . . .

Velvl See how she begs for him the thief!

Izzy The *ganev*!

Zlatke I gave him food then so that he shouldn't steal it . . . From the cradle on he had to feed himself, my milk, his, I had to sell, before he was even born, to the Zokhliner's grandchild, I sold his milk. *(crying)* I fed a strange child while mine lay at home in misery.

Reb Meyer Oy, it's the truth, oy, it's the truth, I once lived with them in the cellar. When the child started to cry, the beams shuddered from his howls. I used to take a stick of sugar, wrapped in a rag, and give it to him in his mouth, he should think that it was his mother's breast, but he wouldn't let himself be fooled, under no circumstances did he want the little rag. Oy, how he howled, oy, how he howled . . .

Zlatke *(crying)* What could he do, I had no food to give him. Like a deserted chick he had to worry about himself alone before he knew how to speak, while he was still crawling on all fours he had to search for crumbs, like a little chick has to peck . . . What could he do, seeing children eat, *khap*, and swallow, he was hungry. Did you worry about him? Did you give him food that you should beat him now?

Velvl I should tear out my heart for The Blind Perl, I have my own worries, he can drag him out alone. *(exits)*

Berish If someone robbed Efraim, it's a big fat payback on his head, and who cares, the boots all the same just sit there rotting in his shop. Come, Jews. *(goes away from the bed)*

Blind Perl	You will not drag out the kid? No, Yids, no?
Fruma-Leybtshe	She won't let us. *(looks at Zlatke)*
Blind Perl	She won't let us, I will show her that she will yes let us. *(goes to her)* Away from there! *(pushes her away)*
Zlatke	*(wrestling with him)* I will not let you harm my child. Jews, have mercy, have mercy. *(Blind Perl wants to hit her with the sheath of his sword)* Beat me and I won't go away.
Izzy	Why should he beat her?
Shprintse	Right. So why should he beat a Jewish woman? He takes already ten gilden a week and a challah from us. If some-one steals, what business it is of his? Why should he mix in, why?
Berish	Jews, I have an idea, we need to make him blind. Give some-thing a donation. *(collects small change)* Give only something a donation.

The Jews cobble together a small sum. The official looks on with one eye. They give him the money.

Berish	Please here you have it and become blind, don't see and don't hear, become a blind Perl.
Blind Perl	*(takes the money and closes one eye)* Done, I am already blind. The Blind Perl. If you want a thief here, how's that my business? Have him in health, I am already blind. *(wants to leave)*
Efraim	Panya Natsholnik, what are you doing, he slaughtered me, he ruined me in the middle of a sunny day, my boots, my flesh, and my blood! *(runs after the official)*

Blind Perl *(scowling at him)* My boots, my flesh, and my blood. What do you call what you have in your shop? Boots are here for people to wear, not to rot away on display in the shop. *(exit)*

Shprintse He is right, The Blind Perl, oy, he is right. *(exit)*

All exit. Pause.

Zlatke *(calling under the bed)* Crawl out already, crawl out, into the earth you should crawl. *(Motke crawls out)* Because of you, I endure such humiliations and insults, people come suck out my blood. *(she falls on him and beats him and pushes him)*

Motke *(stands and lets her)* Hit me, kill me, do what you want, I won't talk back to you, Mama, I will let you.

Zlatke A curse on all my years, why do I beat him still? The boy wanders around on the streets like a dog, hungry and cold, and I still beat him . . . Look at the state of you, what will be the end of you? *(goes into the kitchen, looks around, and gives him food)*

Motke I don't want to eat.

Zlatke You are hungry, they chased you like a rabid dog.

Motke I am not hungry. I am going to go away from here, I won't be here anymore. I will go, I know already where I will go.

Zlatke Where will you go? Into your grave? You are still just a young child. Who will look after you, who will be your mother?

Motke I know already what I will do, don't worry, Mama, I am a big boy, I'll give it to them. *(makes a fist in the air)* Mama, I will always think of you, wherever I will be, I will think of you, and when I am big and I have a lot of money, I will come

105

back to you in a carriage with two horses, I will come for you, I won't take Daddy, only you.

Zlatke Where will you take me, to my grave, what are you babbling, what? Take off your jacket, I will sew it, look at the state of you. *(she takes his jacket off of him)* Why do you jump over all of the buildings and walls like a wild goat, what will be your black end?

Motke Mama, don't worry, you will see, what I will do yet . . . I will show them who Motke is, I will go out into the world, I will try hard and I will become rich and I will come back to you in a carriage with two horses.

Zlatke Oy, a curse is on me, your father is coming! Hide, he will kill you if he sees you in the cellar. He warned me that I should not let you pass the doorstep, *nu*, crawl under.

Motke crawls into a corner; she covers him and sits fixing his jacket. Leyb is a big, strong young man, blind in one eye, with a rope under one arm.

Leyb *(shouting from the door)* Did you let that *mamzer* into the cellar again? *(looks around)* I warned you that you should not allow that bastard even on the stoop. Where did you hide the boy this time?

Zlatke What do you want, that he should have nowhere to run to, they chased after him like a rabid dog, he ran to his mother. What do you want—I should throw him out, so that they should kill him. You don't want to live to see that.

Leyb *(furious, shouting)* You raised *mamzers, ganevs,* and you hide him still. Where is the boy?

Zlatke He isn't here anymore, he ran away.

Leyb	*(tearing the pants)* What are you sewing? Where is the boy? I will kill him on the spot once and for all!
Zlatke	I don't know where the boy is, what do you want? It's not enough that strangers chased him, now his own father?
Leyb	You still take him in, you've raised quite a thief, just like your own family. *(raises his hand to her)*
Motke	*(watching the entire scene, runs out of his corner with a stick)* I will not let you beat Mama, I will give it back to you! You can beat me yes, my Mama no, won't let you, won't let you. *(holds the stick high)*
Zlatke	*(screaming)* Motke, what are you doing? You'd raise a hand to your own father?
Leyb	*(taking off his belt)* You *oysvarf!* Get out of my house this minute. I will split your head in two. *(wants to beat him)*
Zlatke	*(standing between them)* Go, Motke, go where you want to go, into the big world, you have no father, you have no mother, you were born an orphan in this world. Maybe you will find another mother and father. Go my child. *(cries)*
Motke	Don't cry, Mama, I know already what to do. I will always remember you, Mama. *(wants to go)*
Zlatke	Wait, my child, take this coat with you, and this little bit of bread . . . *(gives him what little bread she has in the house and his pants)*
Motke	*(puts the pants over his shoulder and the piece of bread under his arm)* Be well, Mama. Don't cry, Mama. *(exit)*
Zlatke	My child! My poor child!

END PROLOGUE

ACT ONE

A room in a hotel in a small city, with makeshift beds. Various red and striped scarves in the style of gypsies are draped around the room. A red parrot hangs in a cage, a blush paper lamp is in the middle of the room, two small windows. Dark in the evening.

Alter Terakh, the director of the circus, lies sprawled on one of the beds, his medallions beside him. He is shirtless, wearing red tights, with a thick red velvet sash around his waist and heavy black boots. Mary, the acrobat, sits in a corner in front of a mirror, brushing her hair with the parrot above her. Motke stands and looks at Mary . . . Before the curtain is raised, we hear a Russian song.

> Thousands I have loved
> Thousands I have lost.
> Only one of all of them
> I cannot forget.

Terakh Listen, *Hispanisher Tshampion*, do a trick and pull off an old maestro's boots, show me what you got. If you're caught by Miss Syphilis over there while he, Kanarik, is still yowling like an old tomcat, his yellow curls tufting on his head like a cock's . . . Mary, I am afraid he will hunt Kanarik into the ground, I should live to be hunted into the ground . . . *(turns on his other side and speaks to himself)* Once upon a time to pull a pair of boots off an old whoremonger, you needed a champion—a champion *(snores, breathes heavily until he is snoring loudly)*

Motke *(meanwhile, standing and looking bright eyed at Mary, turns on one foot and points with his finger)* Also take off?

Mary stretches out her leg. Motke kneels down, takes her foot, and removes her slipper; while stroking her foot, he speaks enraptured.

Motke Like a little dove, like a little birdie, a baby one, that I used to catch when I was a little boy—it is so alive, trembling—warm, with feathers. *(bringing her foot to his heart)*

Mary Get lost. Kanarik will come in, see you holding my foot, and he will kill you on the spot.

Motke Kill me? Of Kanarik I have no fear. You saw today how I nailed him wrestling in the street. I had him so long by the neck he had to give up.

Mary He let you win because you're the kid—hey, it's always prettier when the younger one nails the older. Right?

Motke Let me? He didn't let me. I am not afraid of anyone. I'm stronger than God.

Mary Kanarik will slap you up, just like he slaps me.

Motke He *shlogs* you?

Mary Does he *shlog* me? All the time, if I won't do what he says or he sends me somewhere away where I don't want to go.

Motke Where does he send you?

Mary You know already where he sends me. *(pushes him off)*

Motke He *shlogs* you?

Mary Black and blue he made on me, see? *(shows him her arms)* With his belt and he always kicks me.

Motke He *shlogs* you?! That fu . . . My little dove, my little birdie, my little one, I will kiss away your bruises. The syphilis should rot him. My little little birdie, how you spring with your little little feet. When I watched you today how you jumped with your little feet over the wire, my heart beat so, I was so afraid. I would fall off, I should break my hands and feet only that you, that that should never happen to you, never ever. My little bird, my little one, I will cover your little handles in kisses. *(kisses her body all over, her belly, her hands and feet.)* So soft, just like a pillow, like feathers, like a little baby bird's . . .

Mary   *(pushes him off)* Beat it! Beat it! Kanarik will come, and me and you will be dead.

Motke   Don't be afraid, I told you. Kanarik, I'll twist off his head if he does anything to you . . . Mary, listen to me, do you want that we should be good friends like always, forever, nothing should come between us, we will always, always be good friends? I will look out for you, I won't let anything bad happen to you. Tell me, do you want it, do you want it?

Mary   *(eagerly)* And you won't *shlog* me like Kanarik?

Motke   Me *shlog* you? The syphilis should take me, here, the plague, on the spot if I would do anything bad to you. I will cover your beautiful hands and feet with kisses. I will be a true friend to you, *nu*, tell me, do you want it? Give me your hand.

Mary   Shut up, shut up. Kanarik told me that he would take me away from here. He will bring me to Varshe, he said. He said he would bring me into one of the houses where you dance all night and are so beautifully dressed, like the rich ladies dress, where the cavalry come. Such rich horsemen come and dance with the ladies. In such a house he wants to bring me.

Motke   And you want to go with him?

Mary   Yes, I want to be in a house like that where everything is beautiful, filled with light, music always playing, with gorgeous ladies dressed in fancy gowns, I want to dress like, like a gypsy girl with a pair of big gold hoops in my ears and a tiny little dress. Oh, it'll be great, the whole world will be jealous, it'll be great. I don't want to be with Alter Terakh any more, shlepped around the marketplace, showing myself to the drunk goyim who don't even buy me not even one little dress. I want to go to Varshe.

Motke   But I will not let you go with Kanarik. I will run away with you, I will bring you to Varshe. I will buy you beautiful dresses and make you up like a gypsy, I will bring you to the rich mansions where the music always plays, I, I!

Mary   Ha ha ha. You? You will bring me, who are you? Motke, do you have a pass to travel to Varshe? You don't have a pass, Kanarik has a pass, Kanarik has money, Kanarik is a grown man, a strong man.

Motke   *(crying out)* But I will not let you go with Kanarik, I will smash Kanarik's head in and I will not let you go with Kanarik as sure as I am a Jew, I will not let you. I will take Kanarik's pass and with me you will travel with me, if not I will *shlog* you, bam, with my hand. *(makes a fist)* Say it, him or me? Say it!

Mary   *(smiling)* But do you love me? Do you love me passionately?

Motke   You, I kiss your feet like a little bird, a tiny chick with little feathers I hold you in my hand.

Mary   And you'll kill Kanarik and take his pass? *(he nods his head yes; she runs her hand through his hair)* I loved you from the moment I first saw you and Kanarik, I hate him.

Motke   *(taking up her foot)* My soft, soft, baby dove. *(kisses it; voices are* *heard off)*

Mary   Leave me alone, Kanarik is here.

Motke   I will not leave you.

Mary   He will kill me.

Motke   We will see!

Mary   Shh . . . Motke, later, later, not just yet. *(tears herself away from him)*

Kanarik   *(comes in with a little boot in his hand)* You dressed? Der Pawn is coming, he'll play cards, drink beer. Hurry, put on the rings, you will dance the Russian dance.

Mary   I don't wanna dance, my feet hurt from the wire already. I wanna to go to sleep.

Kanarik   What are you? A married woman? Put on the rings!

Mary   I hate Der Pawn, he reeks of schnapps.

Kanarik   Der Pawn has *gelt*, you can pull some groschen off him.

Mary   I don't wanna!

Kanarik   You dressed? *(lifts up the whip at her; Motke runs to her)* Why are you here? Why aren't you out watching the horses?

Motke   I don't want to watch the horses. I want to be here. I know already who to watch . . .

Kanarik   *(angry)* Go, *mamzer*, go! Got it?

Motke	I don't want to go.
Kanarik	Hunh? Baiting an old whoremonger . . .
Mary	*(waking Alter Terakh)* Alter Terakh, Alter, look what's happening . . .
Alter Terakh	*Ganevs!* Heathens, snakes, gluttons, fire *shlingers*, get out of here, you . . . What? You'll make scandals here? *(stands between them)*
Kanarik	Der Polisher Pawn is coming, a big guy, it'll be a nice living, he won't let our little mouse get dressed.
Alter Terakh	*Ver?* The Polish Pawn? Ah, he is one of my oldest customers. To every city, he follows me to admire my artistry. I'll give you a *shvartse yor, ganevs*, heathens, fire *shlingers!* *(to Mary)* *Di minut* put on the rings with the gypsyishy costume, and you, you little cock eater, why are you standing there? Take the drum with the whistles, you will accompany her, it's an important guest, we can *khap* a pretty groschen. Let me just put on my medallions.

Mary winks at Motke that he should obey, puts the rings on her hands and ears with the gypsy kerchief. Motke stands there furious; Kanarik goes out.

Mary	*(runs to Motke)* Shut up, not a word, today, tonight, we will run away.

Kanarik leads in the gentleman.

Alter Terakh	*(goes to him)* Ah, *wilkomen, wilkomen*, Pawn! I present to you, without further ado, *avec plaisir*—my daughter. Oh, already, such a long wait for you. *Au jourd'hui*, we have something for you completely new, *gants nay*—yes, such that you have never seen before. My daughter will now dance the *Rusishe*

tants . . . Nisht vor, my little dove, *mayn . . . mayn . . .*

Der Pawn (*sizing up Mary*) Felicitation, you beautiful *fraulein*, the entire city is mad for you. In the casinos, the pawns drink to your beautiful legs . . . Ah, dear Pawnie Katrinash! You have an acrobat, the only one like in the world, in Varshe you wouldn't even see such a one.

Alter Terakh Cavalry men, officers travel long distances to see her artistry. Wherever she appears, men go *meshuge* for her. With my daughter, I can show her off to best of the kaisers, *presidentes*, and kings . . . *Ot*, a cavalry officer wrote her a letter. I carry it here by my heart. (*takes out a letter*) A love letter he writes to her: *Ti moya mila ya*, you are my beloved . . . *Drogaya golubtsik,* my dearest dove, he writes to her . . . So writes a lieutenant general to my daughter and what chocolate and flowers he sends to every city, thither and hither, no place left to store them. She eats only *shokolad.* Anything else she can't digest.

Der Pawn I have also brought her something of the best sort, beautiful acrobat. I have the great honor of presenting you with the *shokolad* as a sign of my enormous respect for her as well as this bottle of perfume, it comes from the best perfumers in Paris . . . And also you gentlemen, I have not forgotten. I know that you are not averse to the drop of the old bitters. This bottle of cognac is for you—the organ grinder's eldest son, you, I did not know what to choose for you, please take this *gelt* and choose something for yourself. (*gives Kanarik money*)

Alter Terakh And for my other son, you did not bring anything? He will be *broygez . . .*

Der Pawn Ah! For the Spanish Champion, I know, I know, he has worked hard. *Nu*, take this, please, and choose for yourself something, and don't be *jaloux*. (*gives Motke money*)

Alter Terakh	*(to Motke, who has not taken the money and instead turned away)* See, *ganev*, what's on the line? The Pawn is my oldest customer, you'll drive him away from me, take the money or a *shvartse* pox on all your houses.
Mary	I will take it for him, I will give it to him later. *(takes it)* Motke, soon . . . *(winks at him)*
Alter Terakh	*Nu, khevre,* now a little *shtik* for the pawn. Extravaganza.
	They beat a Russian dance on the drums, Mary dances, they sing, the gentleman sits and kvells.
Kanarik	*(to Motke)* Get outta here, they need to be alone. *(Motke does not move)* Hey *mamzer*, duh, they need to be alone!
Motke	I don't want to go.
Kanarik	*(to Terakh)* The *mamzer* doesn't want to go, there'll be a *skandál.*
Alter Terakh	The Pawn is an outstanding Christian. You want I should throw him out, look, they need to be alone, come.
Motke	I do not want to go!
Alter Terakh	A *brokh* on all my years! *Mamzer, gey,* you want to destroy me? Come, already, come.
Kanarik	*(to Terakh)* Get him. Why are you standing there? *(He winks at Terakh; both of them take Motke)*
Alter Terakh	*(taking Motke) Nu,* come, Motke, come make some money. *(both drag him off)*
Motke	*(while they are dragging him off, shouts)* I do not want to go. I do not

want to go. *(they drag him away)*

Der Pawn   Well, so, I will be the lady's *liebchen*, please, *pawnyenkeh*, sit down over here. *(pats his knee)* I want to show you some-thing.

Mary   *(turns away from him)* What's your hurry? . . . What do you want to show me?

Der Pawn   A pretty thing. *(pulls her down on his knees)* Like *this!* *(kisses her)*

Mary   *(wiping her cheeks)* Your moustache is moldy.

Der Pawn   *Di pawnyenkeh's* making fun of me. *Di pawnyenkeh* is not treating me well. *(wants to give her another kiss)*

Mary   *(turns away from him)* Like I told you, your moustache is moldy. *(runs away from him)*

Der Pawn   *(runs after her and cannot grab her)* I know how to catch a chickie. I know already how to catch a little bird chick. I am an ex-perienced hunter. You put food in the net. *(takes out his wallet and takes out some paper money)* And the little chickie will come all by herself into the net. *(whistles at her and sings)* Come, come, little birdie, come into the net. *(Mary goes toward him slowly, she wants to grab the money, he grabs her)* O, that's how you catch a little chickie, that is how. *(kisses her)*

Mary   But the little chickie is so tired. *(lies on him)* She has such tired little feet. *(puts her feet on him)* *Nu*, and now, pawn, bend over and close your eyes. If you promise me that you won't look, I will show you something.

Der Pawn   Will it be worth it?

Mary   Very.

Der Pawn   All right, then, I am almost blind. I don't see. I abandon my-self to the mercy of *di pawnyenkeh*, I do as *di pawnyenkeh* says. *(Closes his eyes. Mary sticks her hand under his shirt. He laughs.)* You're tickling me.

Mary   I didn't want to; you peeked.

Der Pawn   I cannot see a thing. *Swovo honoro!*

Mary   No. I will blindfold you so that you can't see.

Der Pawn   Why?

Mary   I'm ashamed.

Der Pawn   If *di pawnyenkeh* is ashamed, that is something else. Blind-fold me.

Mary   *(blindfolds him)* Can you see?

Der Pawn   *Swovo honoro*, nothing. *(she sticks her hand into his breast pocket)* O, that really tickles me . . .

Mary   And that is not all. We're just getting going, baby. The best part's for later, but first you gotta swear to me that you don't see.

Der Pawn   *Swovo honoro*, I don't see.

Mary   O, I believe you. *(takes his wallet from his pocket and hides it between her breasts)* But if you're looking, I don't want to do it.

Der Pawn   *Swovo honoro*, I cannot see.

Mary   Soon, just one more minute. *(she sticks out her foot on his bald head and strokes him)* Does that feel good?

Der Pawn   Very, what are you doing that with?

Mary   It is a game called "Piggie and Birdie." The birdie goes up the piggie's back. *(she crawls on top of him)* Do you like it?

Motke appears at the window; he waves his fist at her, and she throws him the wallet with the money.

Mary   Stash that; we will run away together tonight.

Der Pawn   *(hears voices, pulls off the blindfold)* Who's there?

Motke   *(goes toward him)* Get out of here. This minute out. *(wants to hit him)*

Mary   O please, God, Der Pawn will scream, run! *(she pushes him out though the window)*

Motke   *(off)* Wait, I want to slap that goy's bald head red.

Der Pawn   What's he doing here? I paid already.

Mary   Shush, come here, let's play some more Piggie and Birdie, *nu*, bend over.

Der Pawn   I don't want to play anymore. What did he want? Why did he come back in? This is not an honest business here, you people do not handle your guests properly. *(looks in his pocket)* Where is my money? Who filched my money? Aha, you blindfolded me and took my money. *Karaul!* Guards! *Politsey*! I am running straight to the police . . . People! People! My money, give it to me this minute!

Mary   What money? What are you talking about? What do you want, Pawn? You're drunk, what money?

Der Pawn   The money you gave away to your lover. *Politsey!* People! People!

Alter Terakh and Kanarik run in.

Alter Terakh   What's going on here? What's happened? *Shvayg!* In the name of God, Pawn, *shvayg!* They will close my business.

Der Pawn   Yids, kikes, thieves! What do you take me for? She tricked me, all my money gone. Three hundred rubles, sucked out of me and passed on to her lover. I am going now to the police! I will show you!

Alter Terakh   What police? When police? Shut up! Pawn! *(to Mary)* Mary, love, my child, where is the money? Give me the money, that's not nice if you took the money. *Gib op dos gelt!*

Der Pawn   She passed it on to her lover.

Kanarik   Who? Me?

Der Pawn   I don't know who her lover is; it seems there was another one here.

Kanarik   Motke. *(runs out with Terakh and brings in Motke)*

Alter Terakh   Motkele, my child, *gib op dos gelt.* That's not nice if you took the money from der pawn.

Motke   What money? I don't know nothing about no money.

Der Pawn   I am going to the police, right now to the police!

Alter Terakh   What police? The police know about people like you, that approach a respectable *fraulein* and make a whole *bilbl* on her that she took money from them . . . My daughter took money from you? . . . Cavalry officers write to her love letters . . . Here you have it, *(throws a box of chocolates at the pawn)* the chief of police, chocolates he sends to her, she will take your money? Daughter *mayne*, did you take money from der pawn?

Mary I didn't take no money. I don't know what he wants from me, der pawn.

Alter Terakh You see? Who are you, pawn? What are you doing here? Why did you come here in the middle of the night and throw yourself at my daughter? Police! *(goes out and shouts)* *Politsey! Policia! (comes back)* What are you looking for here? Why did you attack my child? My innocent, poor child, she took money from you? The chief of police is in love with her, writes her love letters and now you dare say she stole money from you! Why are you attacking us? *Politsey!* *Di minut* come to the police . . . Do you have a pass? I have a pass, do you have a pass? *Politsey* . . . I will have you sent to Siberia, seven years hard labor. You attack my daughter in the middle of the night, wanting to hurt her! Look, people, look, *gevald*, rape, rape, he's hurting my child, *politsey! Di minut* come to the police. *(shouting)* *Politsey!*

Der Pawn *Yid*, what are you talking about? What are you saying, what?

Alter Terakh *(shouting)* *Politsey!* A man attacked us in the middle of the night, I will not let him go, to the police, come *di minut*. *(Der Pawn wants to go away)* You will not run away from me! You will not escape to the police, you must go. *(Der Pawn tears himself away and runs, Terakh shouts after him)* This is payback from all the Jews . . . *Nu*, now. *(to Motke)* Listen up, *mamzernik*, give me the money; if not I will do to you like I did to the goy, as I am a Jew, I will give you up to the police. You don't have no pass from me, and who your father is I don't know either . . . it'll be ugly!

Motke	Let it be ugly, do I look worried? Give me up to the police, I will tell them you sell the girl to drunks for money and when she says no, you beat her. We will all sit in jail, it will be just like home.
Alter Terakh	What are you saying? What have I lived to see?
Kanarik	*(to Mary)* Ha ha ha! Look at that, o the little traitor that came running after us, o the little geek that bites the heads off the chickens, o that's who you infected with money, my little tightrope walker, my little artiste. *(goes to hit her)*
Motke	*(jumps at him)* Just touch her, let's see you touch her, you'll be a dead man on the spot.
Kanarik	What? You won't let me? O, so you get the first slap! *(hits him)*
Motke	*(jumps back at Kanarik, grabs him by the neck)* I will leave you a dead man.
Alter Terakh	*(hits them both with his cane)* Just my luck! Heathens, *ganevs!* What are you doing? *(to Mary, who is looking with delight at Motke strangling Kanarik)* Gedenk in got, tokhter, separate them. Why are you just standing there?
Mary	*(as if something finally dawned on her, runs to separate them, to Motke)* Hand over the money, come on, hand over the money!
Motke	*(confused)* What money?
Mary	The money from the goy that I threw out to you. *(to Kanarik)* I thought that it was you when he came through the window so I threw it to him . . . Hand over the money!
Kanarik	*(triumphant)* You hear, *ganev!* *(to Mary)* You thought it was me? *(takes her)* You hear what she said, thief! Hand over the money;

she wanted to give it to me.

Mary   Yes, you, my *khosn*.

Kanarik   You hear, you hear?

Motke   *(stunned)* You thought that I was him? Your *khosn*, you thought, huh? Not me but Kanarik? Who has the red face, ha? You gave away the money to me . . . Good, good, I'll give you back the money. *(to Kanarik)* Go outside to the stable, I hid it in the horse's saddle, take it. I don't want it.

Kanarik   The money is in the saddle, you thought that it was me, come on, Alter!

Alter Terakh   What a thief! What a . . . He thought he'd get away with it.

Kanarik and Alter Terakh exit.

Mary   Shut up, Motke. You will get the money back. *(Motke looks at her)* I love you, I want to go away with you.

Motke   Go to Kanarik . . . You thought that it was him when you gave me the money, you said it yourself.

Mary   I was just saying that so Kanarik would think that I love him. Because I want to convince him that he should run away with me tonight.

Motke   What has it got to do with me, go if you want. *(pushes her away from him)*

Mary   Motke, I love you, I want to go away with you, you don't have a pass, Kanarik does, take his pass with the money and run away with me.

Motke   Kanarik will give us up.

Mary   Make it so that Kanarik should not give us up to the police. That Kanarik should disappear. You can . . .

Motke   How? What do you mean?

Mary   (takes out a soldier's knife and gives it to him) Wait up for us at night in the woods, I will convince Kanarik he should run away with me. We will hide in the woods tonight by the black river, wait for us there and make it so that Kanarik should disappear, and that you should be called Kanarik . . .

Motke   (trembles, the knife falls from his hand) Mary!

Mary   (picks up the knife and gives it to him) I love you, I want to be with you, only with you alone. You should do with me what you want, *mayn tayere*, because I love you . . .

Motke   (pulls her to his heart) Mary!

Mary   Kanarik, my beloved!

Motke   (*puts his hand over her mouth*) Shhh, *Shvayg!*

They move away from one another while staring at each other.

CURTAIN

ACT TWO

Café Varshe. A coffee house in Warsaw in the old city. Red lights burn out front. Twilight. The room reeks of cheap perfume. A figure is asleep in half light on the couch. A couple of girls sit and speak among themselves. They are half dressed in revealing white blouses and short petticoats with bright blue, red, or black stockings and very high heels. Their hair is long and loose or tied back with a red ribbon. Behind a buffet full of cheese, cakes, eggs, and other edibles sits a girl, Khanele, of about 18 or 19 years old, properly dressed with her hair in two long braids, reading a novel. Hindl, the owner of the cafe, stands speaking with the girls. Basha folds newly purchased linens, bed sheets, blankets, and handkerchiefs. She is a healthy looking girl. She is sitting at table with the other prostitutes.

Basha   Look at these coverlets, I bought them to decorate the beds, I love when everything is white in the house . . . See, Hindl, how strong the linen is, you're sort of a connoisseur, right?

Hindl   *(tries to tear it with her teeth, cannot)* Pure weave . . . But why did you buy all of these at once? Does this mean you are getting married then, that you're packing up your trousseau?

Basha   And if I don't get married, I can't purchase whites . . . I have an entire hope chest already.

Hindl   The linens will rot there in your chest—for what? It's all the same, you're not going to get married. In my opinion, you should sell the linens. I should like to have a trousseau for my Khanele.

Basha   Would you look at that, her one can collect for a trousseau, and we can't, how does she know that I won't get married? If God wants it, anything can happen.

The Girl from Zokhlin   She doesn't have the right? You mean that only Khanele can put together a trousseau. *(goes to Basha)* Basha, use them with your *bashert* in happiness and health.

Red *(who has been sitting the whole time in black silk laying down cards)* Basha, don't worry, your destined one will come. *(shows the card)* See, see, he's coming, *(turns over another card)* but every time he shows himself, the ace of spades stands in his way, *(turns over another card)* but the queen she protects him, she follows him like a good angel and protects him. *(turns over another card)* There again the ace of spades, *oy vey* . . .

The Girl from Zokhlin What is the ace of spades, then?

Red *(earnestly)* It is death; when that card appears, so does death.

The Girl from Zokhlin *Oy vey*, where do you know that from?

Red A *kishef-makherin*, a sorceress, taught it to me when I was a little girl. The ace of spades always appears before a catastrophe. Before my mother died and when Dovid Kamanshik abandoned me, both times the ace of spades showed up.

Basha And then what happened? Oy, tell, tell . . .

Hindl Please, come on, people who believe in witchcraft are fools. *(to Zokhlin)* See to it, love, that she sells me her linens; what does she need them for? She has no use for them, and my Khanele would have a trousseau. *(winks at Zokhlin)*

The Girl from Zokhlin And I just don't really know why you collect linens in a chest to begin with. *Meyle*, buying a little hat—now that I understand, you want a little treat, silk stockings, but linens? That's all right for a good girl, for Khanele, but for us? One black year we all gave away our souls to the devil, fuck it . . .

Red *Oy*, Basha, sell Khanele the linens already, it will be so beautiful, there will be a wedding. *(to Hindl)* Oy, I just love a wedding so much, I have never ever even been to a wedding, *oy*, I'd love to go . . . Sell the linens, Basha, and there will be a wedding.

Hindl You see, everyone is telling you to sell the linens so Khanele will have a trousseau. In any case, they'll never be of use to you.

Basha Even if I was certain that they'd rot away in my chest, that the mice would devour them, I still wouldn't sell. *(angry)* Khanele herself is only a girl, I am also a girl, I will have a trousseau. *(everyone laughs)*

The Girl from Zokhlin She is a girl . . . She wants to have a trousseau . . . Sister, it's hopeless, beat that *narishkeytn* outta your head.

Basha Over all your asses, we have a God in heaven and if he wants, he can make anything happen. *(the girls laugh harder)*

The figure on the couch awakens; even in the darkness you can see the shine on his boots.

Red Oh, Kanarik!

The Girls Kanarik, Kanarik!

The figure steps into the light, his black mane tousled, his face brooding and sullen; he rubs his eyes, momentarily unsure of his surroundings. It is Motke, a few years older, wearing a velvet suit and a gold watch. He glances over at Khanele, to the girls.

Motke Why are you laughing? The lamps are lit, it's already dark.

Red Oh, Kanarik, I turned over the ace of spades again, I'm scared that something bad's gonna happen.

Motke   Let me rest. *(glances at Khanele with love, goes over to the buffet)*

(Khanele is absorbed in her book)

Hindl   *(from the corner)* Khanele, you don't hear? *Oy vey,* the *kinder* will be here soon, let me go in, I have nothing prepared. *(exit)*

Khanele puts down her paperback, pours a glass of tea, serves Motke and Red, then sits back down to read some more. Motke looks at her.

Red   *Oy,* how fine you look dressed in that tight red shirt with the fringes. You look like a rich man, like a real royal. A whole day I pressed that shirt so it would be as stiff as a board, see what kind of a hand now I've got from pressing. *(she gestures with her hand)*

The Girl from Zokhlin   *(an aside to Basha)* Look how she pretties him up, come on, look . . . Too bad his *kala* Mary isn't here, she'd gouge that one's eyes out.

Basha   Are you jealous because Kanarik makes love to her?

The Girl from Zokhlin   Me jealous of her? What do I care for men? If I wanted to pretty him up, you'd soon see what kind of hat he'd buy for me.

Basha   So why don't you dress him, then?

The Girl from Zokhlin   Because I don't want to, look, look, look how she's decked out . . . Still waters dig deep. *(goes over to the table, speaks to Motke flirtatiously)* Oy, King Kanarik. Look at you dressed in a new suit with that gold watch. He looks, you know, just like some magnate: what a *fargenign* to look at him.

Motke   *(looking at Khanele the whole time)* Another glass of tea with *kikh-lekh*. *(to Zokhlin)* Sit down!

Red   To make that suit for him, I had to pay the tailor 25 rubles for that.

The Girl from Zokhlin   Everything she made, the suit, the shirt. Maybe she also gave birth to Kanarik?

Red   Yeah, everything me. His cravat I embroidered with my own hands. I shined up his spatterdashes so that he would look fine. Isn't that right, Kanarik?

Motke   Right, right. *(looking at Khanele)*

The Girl from Zokhlin   Look at that, look at that. *Oy*, Mary will gouge her eyes out.

Red   We're going to stroll around tonight, he's gonna take me to the theater.

The Girl from Zokhlin   Just you by yourself? Kanarik will take all of us with him, right, Kanarik?

Motke   *(the whole time looking at Khanele)* Yeah, everyone, everyone!

The Girl from Zokhlin   *(triumphant)* See? See, already you're not the boss of us, what are you, his wife, what? You're just a stupid bagel hole like all of us.

Shlomo, an aging pimp and well known pickpocket, enters. He has a thick red neck, and when he walks his gold chain swings atop his protruding beer-bellied paunch. Close at his heels at all times is his sidekick, Yoinele Malpeh, a short, hook-nosed humpback, faithful as a dog.

The Girl from Zokhlin   *Oy, Mamele-kroyn*, Shloymele's here. *(all the girls want to get up)*

Motke   *(in a commanding tone)* Stay seated!

The girls don't know what to do—they are both titillated and scared.

129

Shlomo	Where are the broads? It's already late in the night and they aren't on the street yet? *(comes over to Motke's table)* Please, look how he sits with his brides, the young groom. Outside, my living is ripped from my hands, and he holds forth with the *kalehs*? Why are you keeping them here? *(to the girls)* *Aroys,* on the street!
Motke	*(angry)* Stay seated. Drink tea, eat *kikhlekh!*
Shlomo	What are you doing here on a black year, for fuck sakes? You don't take any weekly payment for the *kalehs?* Why are you holding them here? *Aroys af der gas!*
Motke	Stay seated!
Shlomo	What is this? *(to the girls)* *Aroys af der gas!*
The Girls	*(frightened)* Kanarik, let us out.
Motke	Your heads, I will split open whoever makes one move from there. Here you will sit with me at the table. Tea, *kikhlekh,* and whoever doesn't like it will get pounded.
Shlomo	*(banging on the table)* My *parnose,* my bread, for my wife and child, you'll destroy me, you don't take any *gelt* from me?
Motke	*(getting up)* Drag the fuck out of here this minute!
Shlomo	*(hitting his heart)* My bread, my flesh, my blood. *(they stare at one another, then attack)*
Basha	*(screams)* *Oy, Mamala-kroyn,* what'll become of us? What'll become of us, Khanele, *oy vey!*
Khanele	*(going over to Motke)* Kanarik, I beg you, do it for me, the guard is by the door, don't make a scandal, let the girls go out.

Motke   *(looks at Khanele, becomes pale)* For you, I'll do anything, otherwise he'd be leaving here without a head, I should live to see it, without a head . . . *Nu*, Shloymele, bitchass, take the girls. *(to the girls) Nu*, out, on the street.

Shlomo   So, *mamzer*, my living he goes and takes away from me. Every groschen he pulls out of me to play house with his brides.

Khanele   I thank you so much, Mr. Kanarik, for doing what I said.

Motke   I only did it for you, I should live like that only for you . . .

Khanele laughs embarrassed, goes behind the buffet, takes out her book. Motke broods awhile and then goes over to her with light steps.

Motke   Khanele . . . Khanele, what are you reading?

Khanele   A story . . .

Motke   A pretty story?

Khanele   Yes, it's called "Yoseleh" . . . It is a story about an orphan who doesn't have a father and doesn't have a mother and people are so cruel to him . . . Do you want it? *(she gives him the book)*

Motke   *(embarrassed)* I can't read, never learned. Do they beat him? Like me, they beat me when I was a little boy . . . I'd like to smash his head in now.

Khanele   What? You didn't have a mother either?

Motke   I had, yes, a mother, she wouldn't let them beat me. Because of that I love her very much, very very much, and you, I also love you.

Khanele	*(shocked and embarrassed)* Me?
Motke	*(covering his mouth)* No . . . I mean my mother, I love her and you also—like my mother . . .
Khanele	*(laughs, surprised)* I don't know what you mean. *(reads further)*
Motke	*(standing, looking at her)* Khanele, I want to tell you something . . .
Khanele	*(puts away the book in angst and looks at Motke with panic)* What do you want to tell me?
Motke	Khanele, do you want to? I mean . . . I want to . . . Khanele, hear me out, I love you very much, like my mother!
Khanele	*(even more shocked, with a forced laughter)* Go you already, why do you love me? You don't have enough to love?
Motke	Khanele, I want to become your husband, truly, I would like to live like that, my mother should live to see it . . .
Khanele	*(panicked)* You don't have enough *kalehs*? You have already so enough girls, what do you want from me? *(wants to go)*
Motke	*(takes her by the hand)* Don't go away, please, don't go away, hear me out, I would never harm you, I should die diseased here on the spot if I ever want to do anything bad to you. Once I wanted to do something *shlekht* to you but I couldn't.
Khanele	*(panicked)* Me, you wanted to do something *shlekht* to me, why?
Motke	When I first saw you, Khanele, I wanted you so much that I wanted to *shlekht* you, I stole into your room at night when you were sleeping in the little alcove . . .

Khanele (panicked) *Oy, Mamele kroyn!* . . .

Motke Only I couldn't do it to you, I saw how you slept, with your eyes closed like a baby chick that closes it eyes because it is afraid that men will hurt it and begs exactly like my mother used to when I was a little boy and I caused her trouble stealing, and she stitched up my trousers, her eyes also gleamed like a little hen's before it is slaughtered; that gave me such a pull on my heart that I wanted to fall on the ground before you . . . I was so quiet, quietly I stole out that you should not hear, not know of anything bad I was going to do . . .

Khanele *Oy, Mamele-kroyn, oy!*

Motke From that moment I have had no peace, I don't know it yet, *(gestures to his head)* I can't bear it . . . If I think of you asleep with your eyes closed, I cannot look at the other girls . . . I long for you, not like for the other girls, no, no, completely different, I want to have a wife, my own wife. And my mother should be with her in the home, running the household, just after the wedding, like any *mentsh*, I want to travel around to all the markets and trade, and she should sit at home and cook dinner. Coming home from the marketplace in a cold frost, throwing off my fur, staying home with my wife, in the house so warm, so good, not like here, not with the girls . . .

Khanele *(the whole time she listened to him in a panic, saying with her hand over her heart)* Why did you choose me, *davke?* You know very well that I am not for you, you know that very well.

Motke Why not? I will throw away the business, I have already thought about giving up the life with the girls, I will become a decent man like all other men, I will handle horses or fish, I will be something completely different, become completely different, I love you . . .

Hindl *(came in earlier unnoticed and overheard)* *Vey iz mir,* Khanele, get into the house! You have something to do there!

Khanele looks at Hindl, jumps up, and exits.

Motke Why are you so afraid of me? I won't do anything to Khanele.

Hindl *(with a forced smile)* Who said *afraid?* Who's afraid of you then? What are you, a murderer? *Kholile . . .* It's kosher, Khanele, had inside in the house something to do.

Motke You have nothing to be afraid of from me, I will do nothing to Khanele, I love Khanele, I really love her.

Hindl What did you say, *vey tsu mir!* *(angrily)* What do you have with Khanele? Why are you obsessing over Khanele? Why, what love?

Motke Hindl, I have a few hundred rubles, I will throw it all away, the girls I will sell to Shlomo. I will become a coachman or a fishmonger. And I want to marry Khanele.

Hindl An angry dream on my enemies' heads, you want to marry who? With my Khanele? *Tfu* that should become, my child is a pure child, and you have nothing to ask of my child, surely you don't think that I have such a desperate living I must deal with a suitor such as yourself, that anyone may have dealings with my child . . . My child is not for such people as you . . .

Motke *(angry)* Who am I? A *mamzer?* I also have a mother. *(slams his hand on the table)*

Hindl *(frightened)* Who said anything about your mother, *kholile,* I know you have a mother, what Jew doesn't have a mother, may she live to a 120, if I have my way.

Motke I only meant . . . It wouldn't be good if you had something to say about my mother . . . It wouldn't be good. *(goes to the door and calls out onto the street)* Hey, girls! Come in here now!

Red *(comes in)* Kanarik, did you call me? *(Shlomo comes running in with Yona Malpeh and a few young punks)*

Motke *(to Red)* Can you write a letter in Yiddish?

Red Yeah, my *bobe* taught me.

Motke Sit yourself down and write me a Yiddish letter, there you have ink and paper, now write. *(takes a pen and paper from the buffet and gives it to her)*

Shlomo Look at this, what does he need you for?

Red So I can write!

Motke Write an opening to a mother, a good mother, *a gute mame.* *(she writes)* Did you write it already?

Red Yep.

Motke Read!

Red *(reading)* "*Tsu mayn libe mame!*"

Motke *Tsu mayn libe getraye gute besteh mame.*

Shlomo Look, what a title, like to a countess, a little jewel, his mother. *(they laugh)*

Motke *(notices it and pretends he doesn't)* And now write this: I am sending to you my beloved mother 25 rubles, there you have them. *(puts money on the table)* And buy yourself a wig, a pair of shoes, and a *shabbes tukh*, don't buy anything for my father, everything is for you, because he used to beat me when I was a little boy.

Shlomo   A shame he didn't bury him when he was still a kid.

Motke   *(pretends he didn't hear)* Did you write that already?

Red   Yep.

Motke   And now write this: "I am in Warsaw, a craftsman, a worker, I am. I learned a trade." *(thinks)* What kind of trade?

Shlomo   Whoring thieving pocket robbers.

Motke   *(pretending not to hear)* I am a fishmonger. I work with fish.

Shlomo   *(jumps in)* With caviar!

Motke: And write on like this, come travel to Warsaw, Mama, I am going to be a *khosn!*

Shlomo: What did he say? Be a *khosn? Mazl tov,* everyone, let's hear it, whose gonna be the *kaleh?*

Hindl   *(from behind the buffet)* A curse is on me, you know. *(turns to Shlomo about Motke)* The kid is *meshuge!*

Motke   Did you write it already?

Red   *(thinking that Motke means to marry her)* Yes, I am going to be a *khosn . . .*

Motke   With a nice Jewish girl, a respectable one. *(Red looks sadly at him in shock)* Write "a respectable Jewish girl."

136

Red *(saying sadly)* A respectable Jewish girl.

Motke *(cutting her off)* Yes, as respectable as you are Mama, like Zlatke.

Shlomo Zlatke is good, if that's her only name . . . You know what she's like with a son like him, as the mother is so is the child, the apple doesn't fall far from the tree.

Motke *(grabs a chair and holds it over Shlomo's head)* What did you say, what, say it over once more.

Shlomo *(with fear)* What did I say? You yourself said, "Zlatke."

Motke My mother, you diddle? *(grabs the man by his neck and points with his finger to the floor)* This is Zlatke's shoes, her nails, feet, down on the ground! On your knees for Zlatke! *(holds the chair over Shlomo's head; Shlomo is afraid, falls on the ground)* Kiss Zlatke's feet, kiss her shoes, just like that you will kiss Zlatke's shoes. *(he pushes his head down until Shlomo's mouth is touching the floor; Motke pushes him away)* Go, you are not ready to kiss Zlatke's shoes.

Motke sits down at a table, sad and thoughtful. A long pause.
Reb Meylekh comes running in out of breath.

Reb Meylekh What happened here? Such *gevalds*, cries I heard, the police will come in, you know, and make me unlucky.

Hindl *(taking him by the arm)* Shvayg, shvayg . . . Der yung iz meshuge. *(quietly about Motke)* He has *davkeh*, a desire to get married to Khanele, no one else.

Meylekh *Mit* Khanele, him? *(quietly)* I am afraid of that *yung*. Hindl, I am afraid, immediately get Khanele out of the house, hide her at her uncle's. *(looking at Motke)* I will quiet him down, get Khanele out of here.

Hindl exits. Meylekh goes over to Motke with a forced friendliness.

Meylekh Why are you sitting here so deep in thought? A young man like you, what? Business is rotten?

Motke *(snaps up, notices Meylekh, folds his hands)* Reb Meylekh, hear me out, I want to marry your daughter.

Reb Meylekh *(calmly)* Why my daughter, exactly; you short a few?

Motke I don't want to be with them anymore. *(looking at the girls)* I want to begin to lead a new life, I will get married to Khanele and lead a life like every other *mentsh*. A fishmonger, I'll become. *(changing his tone, pleading with great emotion)* Why don't you want it, if I should become a *mentsh*, I also have a mama, an honest, good mama, why don't you want it, why?

Meylekh What don't I want? I don't know yet what I don't want.

Motke *(looks at him confused)* What are you saying? Jew, hear me out. *(takes him by the lapel)* I am still a young guy, I can still become someone completely different.

Meylekh Sure, if you want to, why not?

Motke *(with more feeling)* I have a few hundred rubles of my own money, I will take a trade, I will buy a few horses, and I will cart fish from the train. You will see, I will become a completely different man, an entirely other *mentsh*. My mother should live to see it.

Meylekh *(friendly)* Why not? A young man with a few hundred rubles can do a lot, a lot . . .

Motke Then why don't you want it, why?

Meylekh   What don't I want? I don't know yet what I don't want.

Motke   Why don't you want me to get married to Khanele, make a *shidukh?*

Meylekh   Who said that, that I don't want it? How do you know that I don't want it?

Motke   *(astounded)* What are you saying, what? You want it? Yes, you want it? Me and Khanele, marry . . . Hear me out, *Reb Yid;* Reb Meylekh, hear me out; I have a good mother, a dear mama, I always gave her trouble, from my childhood on I did bad to her and she only good to me.

Meylekh   That is very nice, very good to have a mother like that, a *koved* to have such a mother, O, *va!*

Motke   I love Khanele so much like my mother, hear me out, Jew, I will hold her so dear, so pure. I will be so good to my mother for all the *tsores* that I caused her, to be a *khosn* to such an honest, Jewish girl, with a pure . . . I will not keep her here, I will bring her home to my mother for all to see, all should see.

The girls stand around crying.

Reb Meylekh   Why not, why not. If you should become a real *mentsh,* a human being, we will see then, we will speak then.

Motke   *(with joy)* What did you say, what? Khanele, Khanele! *(wants to run into the house)*

Meylekh   *(holds him back)* O, no, not now, Khanele shouldn't see you, afterwards, afterwards, if you become a *mentsh,* a decent human being, get rid of this living, become a fish handler, have a few hundred rubles of your own, come with a *shad-*

khen like any other Jew, then it will be something else, you will bring your mother, to see with whom I am dealing, but not now . . .

Motke Yes, yes, you are right, yes, yes. *(hits himself on the mouth)* After, after, yes, yes, *nu*, Shloymele, did you hear? Buy the girls? Buy them off me, take them, all of them. How much you got? I don't need them anymore.

Meylekh Let me not be here meanwhile, I know nothing from this. *(he exits; the girls cry)*

The Girl from Zokhlin Chased by a curse. What has he gone and done? Let me run after the tightrope walker.

Basha It's all the same to me, this dog or another, one devil.

Red I knew already that today would not be a good day. The ace of spades runs after me like a black fiend; dearest Kanarik, good Kanarik, what have you gone and done?

Shlomo Do you really mean it? You want to get out of the city?

Motke You won't find my bones here no more. I won't cut into your living no more.

Shlomo You won't take no more percentages, none?

Motke I told you I am selling them to you, every one.

Shlomo And Mary the tightrope walker also?

Motke *(realizing)* Mary, the tightrope walker, no, not her . . .

Mary comes in dressed in black behind Zokhlin.

Motke   You will have no rights over her.

Mary   *(to Motke)* What have you gone and done?

Motke   *(takes her to a corner)* Mary, we must separate, I am going away from here.

Mary   Where?

Motke   I am going to get married.

Mary   Why?

Motke   I don't know why. I must, I want to, I cannot do otherwise.

Mary   And what will you do with me?

Motke   With you? Go away from here, I will take you to a circus, to a vaudeville house, you will go back on the wire, you will work and earn money for yourself, just for yourself.

Mary   I don't want to go, I want to be where you are, with you.

Motke   You cannot be with me, I am going to get married to a respectable girl . . . We must separate. Our luck has run out . . .

Mary   *(cries)* Why? I love you so much.

Motke   I know that I am in your hands, that if you want to you can give me over to the police with one word. That I killed a man, that I use a false name, turn me in if you want to, I can't live this life anymore, send me to Siberia, to *katorge*, to the chains if you want, I cannot be here anymore.

Mary   What are you talking about? I will give you up? *Shlog* me, sell me, do what you want with me, I am yours, I love you,

I love you more than she. *(kisses him on his hand)*

Motke *(stroking her hair)* *Shvayg*, Mary, shush, we must separate.

Mary Why? Why can't you have me with Khanele, steal her away, we will be all together. We will give you money, we will love you, both love you.

Motke Shut up or I will *shlog* you! *(holds up his hand)*

Mary I will speak to her about it, I know already how to speak with her, she will agree.

Motke Shut up before I smash you into the ground, what do you mean? Khanele is like you? Get your things together and get out of here, right now.

Mary *(crying)* I will do everything that you ask of me, everything, I love you, I love you. *(exits crying)*

Shlomo *(going over to Motke)* *Nu*, we're doing business? Sell me your *kalehs*? *Zog* how much you want, hundred rubles, 200 hundred, 300 hundred. *(takes out money)* *Na*, here, take it! *(gives him the money)*

Motke *(looks at him wildly)* Take money? Take money for them? From you? No, no! *Na!* *(throws the money in his face)* You will not have control over them! Hey, girls! Basha! Red!

Girls come in nervously.

The Girls What?

Motke This minute, get together your things and get out of here.

The Girls *(terrified)* And go where?

142

Motke	Go home to your mothers, to your fathers, to your brothers, get work, here your bones won't be found. Out of here!

The girls stand confused, looking with panic and uncertainty at Motke, then at Shlomo.

Shlomo	What are you doing? My living, my whole living, my wife and child!
Motke	*(to the girls)* Don't be afraid, I'd like to see who'd stop you, who'd dare stand in your way. *(to Shlomo)* Your head, I'll split open, *farshtanen? (to the girls)* This minute go home to your fathers, to your mothers, home!
Basha	Righteous God, dearest God, you know everything. *(drags her sister)* Do a miracle, my trousseau, I've already prepared. *(exits)*
Red	*(stops crying, looks with longing at Motke)* Most beautiful creature mine, whose shirts will I wash now? Whose shoes will I polish? *(exits)*
Motke	*(to The Girl from Zokhlin)* Why are you standing there? Why aren't you going home?
The Girl from Zokhlin	*(bitterly)* I have no father, I have no mother, I don't know where to go. The street is my home, I will go out onto the street. *(slowly exits)*
Mary	*(comes in, dressed, with her things, looks around)* No one is here? *(falls on her knees in front of Motke)* Motke!
Motke	Shh . . . Don't call me Motke, someone could still hear!
Mary	I love it so much calling you by your old name, let me!

Motke   Will you give me up?

Mary   I am always yours, wherever I will be. I will stand under your window and see where you live, how you live . . . Be happy, Motke mine . . . Why? *Oy*, Motke, it is so lonely without you, so sad . . . Why?

Motke   *(calming her)* Shush, shhh, of course this is our fate, now we must separate, go our own ways. Be *gezunt*.

Mary   Be *gezunt*, Motke, my love, Motke, my only. *(sings helplessly)*

> Thousands I have loved
> Thousands I have lost
> Only one of all of them
> I cannot forget.

Motke stares after her.

CURTAIN

ACT THREE

A respectable home. Preparing for the marriage contract. Meylekh, without his suit coat, helps by setting out plates.

Hindl	*(setting the table)* What a kid he is, whatever he dreams, he does. No one else, only my Khanele he desired, and he gets her.
Meylekh	I thought that I would fool him; in the end he fooled me, he has really improved *der yung*, what can you do! *(with belief)* And I tell you, *mayn vayb,* if that kind of *yung* becomes decent, he is more decent than all the *yunge layt.* You wouldn't recognize him, he goes you know with me to shul to *daven* every *shabbes,* first I thought I'd shake him. But from the beginning, the *yung* really did what I asked of him, he truly means it.
Hindl	What's happened here? A child in a pinafore, he is not going to bring home to you . . . But if somebody like him becomes a human being—he is a *mentsh,* and he loves Khanele more than his own life, he'd let his eyes be plucked out for her.
Meylekh	And *der iker,* don't forget, a few hundred rubles, and Khanele he takes as she walks and talks, he doesn't want not one groschen for her, and who needs to know then from where he has money, it's not written on his pass.
Hindl	I am only afraid of one *zakh. (goes to him and speaks softly)* How do you know that the *yung* will not return to his old *veg*? It pulls you . . .

145

Meylekh *Narishkeytn* . . . What do you mean, that without her, he would have become what he is? *Nishkoshe*, she will make him a *mentsh*, on her you can depend.

Motke runs in with a letter in his hand, dressed like a respectable young groom-to-be.

Motke *Mekhutn*, Reb Meylekh, my Mama *mayne* is traveling here for the marriage contract, *ot* she writes to me . . . Where is Khanele? *(runs off into the second room)*

Meylekh I like that in the *yung* that he loves that mother of his, honor your mother—"*Kavod Ha Am*"—an important *zakh*.

Hindl And who says he doesn't deserve it? A young man lays so deep in the filth and pulls himself up, he must have a good angel in heaven.

Meylekh My wife, you see . . . Shhh . . .

Motke and Khanele enter, speaking to one another.

Meylekh Is the mother-in-law, *mekhuteneste* as she's called here, coming for the wedding contract?

Motke *Yau, Mekhutn, yau, yau*, if I only knew where she was now, I would run after her, I would . . . She didn't write to me how she is coming on the train, on a carriage, if I knew by which way I would take out a stick and run after her with my horse, I don't know, I must sit here and wait for her.

Meylekh You will wait for her here, you know, she is not coming to no strangers. *(winks to Hindl)* *Mayn vayb*, come away, the young people, maybe they want to discuss something before the contract that we should not hear. *(quietly to her)* Come, *mayn vayb*, we'll stand by the door and we will listen to what the *khosn-kala* have to say. We may also know.

Hindl   You are right, *mayn man.* *(exits with Meylekh, stands by the door)*

Motke   *(looks at Khanele with love, suddenly)* Khanele, Khanele, now tell me, do you want to become a bride for me?

Khanele   *Minastam*, it is destined that I should become your *kaleh*, you know that it is God's will.

Motke   Khanele!

Khanele   I will do everything that *Tateshi* and *Mameshi* ask of me, they know, better than me, what is good for me.

Motke   Khanele!

Khanele   I will tell you the truth, I am really very afraid, my heart trembles inside of me.

Motke   Why are you afraid?

Khanele   You know already why I am afraid . . . I am afraid that you will go back on the same path that you were on. How is that life fit for me? It is better that nothing should become of our *shidukh* unless we are together before God and before decent people.

Meylekh   *(from behind the door)* *A gezunt af ir kop,* you hear how she speaks to him?

Hindl: Only one we can rely on, only on her, I said that, you know, to you, earlier, that on our Khanele we can depend.

Motke   *(throws himself on his knees)* Khanele, I would sooner die, kill myself, drown myself, before I'd do anything so bad to you.

	(raises his finger) I will be faithful to you, mine Khanele, you will see. *(cries)*
Khanele	Do not cry, I believe you, if I did not believe you, I would not have become your *kaleh*.
Motke	Then why do you still speak to me so formally?
Khanele	*Nu*, I should already . . .
Motke	I love you, like my mother, tell me, do you love—my mother?
Khanele	Yes, I have ready for your mother . . . *Ot* what I have ready. *(takes out from the dresser a wig with a scarf)* *Ot* the present I have ready. For the *mekhuteneste*, a pretty present?
Motke	*(cries out)* Khanele?
Khanele	And I want the *mekhuteneste* should lead me under the *khupe* with my Mama, the whole time, if not, it will ruin my wedding.
Motke	*(becomes earnest, thinks a moment, looks around)* My name isn't Kanarik. My name is Motke. Call me Motke, I beg you.
Khanele	Motke? Get already go, you're laughing at me, what kind of name is Motke, Motke's good for a *ganev*.
Motke	I am not laughing, Khanele. I took another's name.
Meylekh	*(from behind the door)* What did he say? Let's just listen. *(listens intently)*
Khanele	Why did you take another name? What man takes another name? You're making fun—

148

Motke   I'm not making fun. Hear me out, Khanele, I wanted to tell you earlier, Khanele, I need to tell you everything. Before I go become your *khosn*, I want that you should know everything and you must know everything. If you still want to be my *kaleh* after then it's good, if not, tell me, I will stand up and go away and you will never see my bones here again.

Meylekh   What is he saying?

Hindl   My heart is telling me nothing good, Meylekh.

Meylekh   *Shvayg*, let's hear what he will say.

Motke   Khanele, hear me out. You see, when you spoke earlier about my mother, I saw that you and I are family, *mishpokhe*, and I can tell you everything, trust you completely, hear me out, Khanele; I took another's name from a man who is already gone, who lives no more, and when you call me with his name, it's like you are his *kaleh*, not mine . . . When you call me Kanarik, it cuts me . . . From his grave you call him, and I want you to be my *kaleh*, *zayn mayne, mayne*, Motke's, not Kanarik's.

Khanele   So why do you use a stranger's name? Why don't you use your own name?

Motke   I didn't have no name . . . When I was a little boy, they all beat me, I didn't have what to eat, so I stole and they all beat me, so I ran away from home without a pass and without a name, and when I got older, I saw that a man must have a pass, if not, he is no man at all, he is like a *brodyage*, a tramp, a nobody. Anyone can fuck him, and he can do nothing to nobody, he has to be afraid in front of everybody, I wanted to be like them, like them with their passes . . .

Khanele   And why didn't you go home to your mother?

Motke   I didn't have no home, I didn't have nothing. I schlepped myself around the world until I met up with that man whose name I took, he did bad to me, many, many times, and I couldn't do nothing to him because he had a pass and a name and I didn't, I made it so that I should have his name and his pass. That's how I did it.

Khanele   *(frightened)* What did you do?

Motke   Khanele, I *makht* it so he should disappear from the world once he wanted to take someone who belonged to me, so I packed him . . . I made it so he could not run away . . . So don't be afraid, he won't come back again, he is already hidden good in a river, with a stone tied around his neck . . . Nobody knows of it, but I don't want to use his name anymore, until now it didn't bother me, so I never thought of it, only since I am going to become your *khosn* and you call me with his name, it cuts me, it's like you are not calling me, but him, you are calling him out from the river, he has become your *khosn*, not me, and I want to be your *khosn*, I, Motke, I will travel into the shtetl where I was born, I will give the officials there a lot of *gelt*, a lot of money to the police, and I will get a pass with my own name, I will call myself like my mother called me, Motke, my mother called me Motke.

Khanele sits, terrified, cannot say one word.

Hindl   *(mumbling from behind the door)* *Vey iz mir, vey iz mir.*

Meylek   Shh . . . *shvayg, shvayg* . . .

Motke   *(after a long pause)* You know everything now, everything, *zog*, do you still want to be *mayn kaleh*? Be a *kaleh* with Motke, not with Kanarik? Kanarik is done, dead, buried, I am Motke, I am Motke! *Zog*, do you want to be Motke's bride? Don't be afraid, say no and I am not here, I'll go away, you

150

won't see me anymore. *(wants to go to Khanele; Khanele is terrified)* What are you frightened of?

Khanele   *(frightened)* Why should I be afraid? Aren't you my *khosn?* Should I be afraid of my khosn? . . . I am only frightened of . . .

Motke   *(cries out)* Khanele! Khanele! *(falls on the ground, buries his face in her lap, crying)*

Meylekh and Hindl look out from behind the curtain and wink at Khanele and nod with their heads. Meylekh shows her with his hand that he knows what he has to do. Hindl pinches her cheeks and winks at Khanele that she should send Motke out.

Khanele   *(looks as if she has just remembered something)* Why are you crying, Motke, don't cry, most likely it is just, you know, your destiny, and your destiny is my fate . . . Go out to the outside, look, maybe my *mekhuteneste* is coming, and you know, she won't know the way, go after her.

Motke   *Shoyn,* Khanele, you're right, *ot* I will go *shoyn,* but say to me just one word then I will know that all is good.

Khanele   What should I say?

Motke   *(with longing)* Say to me "Motke"!

Khanele   *(thinks for the blink of an eye in doubt, with tears)* Motke! Motke!

Motke   I will die, I will . . . I will die . . . It is so good. *(exit)*

Hindl   *(enters with Meylekh)* My poor child. *(Khanele falls into her arms and cries)* Why are you crying? Don't cry, my child, be grateful to God that he unburdened himself to you, you are not his and he is no longer yours, a stranger, *a fremder mentsch,* we must throw the little *pekl* out, and then we have nothing to do with this.

Meylekh *(quiet, to Hindl)* Hindl, I am afraid that we are in the middle . . . Did the *yung* do anything *shlekht* to her?

Hindl Where is your mind? May it fall on my enemies' heads, the *yung* was to her like a yeshiva *bokher*, like a rebbe's son, he went around with her.

Meylekh Why is the girl crying? Hindl, I don't like it that the girl is crying.

Hindl Meylekh, go away from me. Leave me alone with my child.

Meylekh *Ver gevor,* Hindl, find out where we stand. Already, after everything, maybe we should shut up? *Ver gevor.*

Hindl Daughter *lebn, zog mir,* don't be ashamed, I am a mother, tell me . . .

Khanele What should I tell you, Mama *lebn?*

Hindl Did he do anything *shlekt* to you?

Khanele Who, Mama?

Hindl *Der yung.*

Khanele No, Mama, he went around with me like a *khosn,* like a yeshiva *bokher,* everything I wanted he did because he wanted to become a respectable *mentsh,* he went with *Tate* every *Shabbes* to shul.

Hindl You see, what are you *plapling* about? The *yung* treated her as respectfully as a yeshiva *bokher.*

152

Meylekh If so, then to the police, this minute to the police! *Politsey!* On his head, on his hands and feet!

Khanele Mama!

Hindl Meylekh!

Meylekh We must throw this burden off from us, throw it off.

Khanele *Mamele kroyn*, what are you going to do?

Hindl Meylekh!

Meylekh Khanele, do you want to destroy us? He will drag us down with him, we must throw this burden off from us, prove to the authorities that we did not know. *(exit)*

Khanele *(crying) Tate*, what are you going to do?

Hindl *Shvayg*, my daughter, *shvayg*, your father knows best what he has to do.

From the steps, Motke's happy voice is heard.

Motke *(off)* Mama, Mama *getraye!*

Hindl *Shvayg*, he's coming, wipe off your eyes, he should detect nothing, now still the *mekhuteneste*, at this fine hour he brings her.

Khanele Mama . . . I cannot look her in the eyes. *(runs off, Hindl follows; Motke enters)*

Motke Khanele, look, just look who is here, my Mama, my Mama! *(leads in Zlatke wearing a Turkish shawl, old, hunchbacked)* Where are they? Khanele! Look, my Mama. *(runs to the door)* Not here, sit

153

down, Mama, let me look at you, what do you look like?

Zlatke See, see, the wonder of God. *(cries)* Who raised you, my Motke, I thought that you were already dead, and now it's like for me as if I bore you again. I thought that you would drink in all the oceans, I thought that you would drown in all the sea, and now I see the wonder of God. Who took care of you? Who brought up my child? See my *nakhes*, see my happiness! A miracle from God! A miracle from God! *(falls on his head and cries)*

Motke *Shvayg*, Mama, *shvayg*, I will die . . . Where is my father? I want that my father should come, yes, he should also come!

Zlatke He did not want to come. "If he only wrote to you, go ahead," he said. "If he wants me to go to his marriage contract, he is not sick, he can come to me," he said . . . *Oy*, he really wanted to go, *nebekh* . . . *Trern* he had in his *oygn* when I sat down in the wagon, but you did not invite him, *mayn kind*, you treated your father badly.

Motke *(remembering)* He beat me. *(laughing)* I will go to him. If he wants me to come, I will come to him with my *kaleh*, I will come and invite him to the wedding. Then he shall see that Motke's still alive! Yes, but where is she? Where are they all? *(calls)* Khanele! Khanele! My mother has come from traveling, *dokh*. *(runs off and drags on Khanele; Khanele wipes her eyes quickly)* See, Mama, this is my *kaleh, mayn tayere eyntsike kaleh*, and this is my old Mama. *(taking both of them around)* My two Mamas . . .

Zlatke *Mayn tokhter*, who could have predicted that I would have such honor from my son, and even more, his bride . . . *Gotenyu*, why is this coming to me? *Mayn kind;* you must have a good star in the sky, God has looked out for you. *(kisses Khanele on the head)*

154

Motke *(taking out the wig and scarf from the dresser)* You see, Mama, this my *kaleh* bought you as a present.

Zlatke Presents from your *kaleh?*

Motke You bought it for my Mama, isn't that true? Khanele?

Khanele Yes, for my *mekhuteneste.*

Motke Put it on, Mama.

Zlatke No, my *zun*, not yet, in the evening by the wedding contract.

Motke I want my Mama should put on her new scarf now that my *kaleh* bought for her already. *(puts on the scarf)* And here, this I bought for you. *(takes out a pair of golden earrings with a chain and puts them on Zlatke)* I want that you should look pretty, you should be rich, a rich *mekhuteneste.* You are Motke's Mama, I want you should look like a lady!

Zlatke *Zet*, the *nakhes*, people that I have lived to see. *(to Khanele)* I thought you knew that he would go under, because he was a *ganev* in his littlehood, shame and humiliation, I had from him, *zet* what became of him, *zet . . .*

Motke And I told you then, Mama, not to cry, because I said I would come back for you in a coach with two pairs of horses . . . Today I came for you and put you in a coach. The other Motke is dead, buried, and a different Motke is born, isn't it true, Khanele? Ask her, Mama, she made me everything, everything, she . . . *(turns to Khanele)*

Zlatke That is you, my child, you were his angel . . . Your little hands I will kiss. *(wants to kiss Khanele's hands, she won't let her)* Because you have freed a poor man's heart . . . Why don't you speak to me, *mayn kind? Vos shvaygstu?*

Motke Are you ashamed of my Mama?

Khanele *(in doubt)* What are you talking about?

Motke Why are you trembling?

Khanele I am so surprised to see your Mama so suddenly the *mekhuteneste*, he spoke, you know, about my *mekhuteneste* so often, he wanted so much to see his Mama . . .

Motke Now if they have me, both of them will have me, with us she will live, the best of what we eat, she will eat, you should take care of her, me, you will call me Motke like at home, Motke, thief. *(to Khanele)* Motke thief, she called me, you know, they said that I will rot in the jails, hang from the gallows. . . You see what kind of *kaleh* Motke has? Motke will travel home to the shtetl with his *kaleh*, go around strolling outside on the streets, arm in arm, on one arm his Mama, on the other his *kaleh*. *(takes her and strolls with them)* It will be a show . . . They will ask, who goes there? And they will say: There goes Motke with his Mama and with that *kaleh* bride of his. Which Motke? Motke Thief? Yes, yes, and go fuck yourself if you don't like it. *Kha-kha-kha.*

A whistle is heard through the window. Motke runs to it, throwing it open.

Mary *(sticks her head in)* *Gedenk in Got.* Run, Motke. They're coming.

Motke Did you give me up?

Mary *(through the window)* Me, no. Them, your *kaleh*.

Motke Liar! *(runs and grabs Khanele by the hand and looks into her eyes)* Say it's a lie. Look me the eye.

Khanele *(with a cry)* I am not guilty, my father.

Motke   Your father, your father.

Zlatke   *Voz iz dos mayn kind?* Why are you so upset? *Voz iz geshen?*

Motke   *(remembering, pulls himself together)* *Gornisht,* Mama, *gornisht.* The merchants are coming, I must go to the market. *(opens the door and calls)* *Mekhuteneste,* Mother-in-law. Look after my mother like she was your own, you hear me? *(Hindl appears at the door, frightened; to his mother)* Go inside, Mama, the *mekhuteneste* is waiting for you. I need to talk something over with my bride.

Hindl   *(to Zlatke)* *Kumt arayn mekhuteneste.*

Motke   *(emphasizing)* Treat her with respect, like your own mother, *gehert?*

Hindl   *(terrified)* *Gehert.* *(exits frightened with Zlatke)*

Motke   *(to Khanele)* Why? Why?

Khanele trembles.

Motke   Don't be afraid, if I wanted to I would have twisted off your head already. I am not gonna do anything to you. Only one thing I want to ask you. *(holds her by the hand)* Why? Why?

Mary   *(through the window)* Motke, they're coming.

Motke   *(throwing Khanele away)* Go! *(calling to Zlatke in the other room)* Be *gezunt,* Mama.

Zlatke   *(enters)* Where are you going my child? Now? At such a time?

Motke   I must go into the world.

Zlatke To where? You leave me here alone?

Motke I will come back for you! Go on. *(kisses his mother and jumps out through the window)*

A group of policemen, led by Meylekh, by the door.

CURTAIN

GLOSSARY

adieu	goodbye
avec plaisir	with pleasure
au jour'dhui	today
arois	out
af der gas	on the street
a shrek angefaln af alemen	a terror on all of us
bashert	destined soulmate
bilbl	false accusation
bobe	granny
broigez	angry
davke	especially, in spite of
daven	pray
der iker	the crux of the matter
Der Pawn	The Gentleman
der yung	the youth
di minut	this minute
dokh	duh
farginign	pleasure
gelt	money
getraye	dear
ganev	thief
gib op dos gelt	hand over the money
gotenyu	my god
gornisht	nothing
farshtanen	understand
fire shlingers	fire swallowers
gedenk in Got	remember God
gehert?	got it?
gants niyes	completely new
gevald	help

gezund	health
goyim	gentiles
gornisht	nothing
groshen	pennies
khevrey	guys
kalehs	brides
khap	grab
kholile	god forbid
khusn	groom
khupe	wedding canopy
koved ha am	honor your parents
kumt arayn	come in
liebchen	love
makht	made
mamashi	mommy
mamzer	bastard
makhutn	father-in-law
mekhuteneste	mother-in-law
mayn tayere	my dear
man	husband
mentsh	human being
meshuge	crazy
mishpokhe	family
mayne	mine
nebekh	pity
Nisht vor?	Not true?
na	here
nu	so
oign	eyes
oysvarf	outcast, infidel
panyenkeh	mademoiselle
pekl	package
plappling	babbling

polizay, policia	police
reb	mister
Rusishe tants	Russian dance
shlog	beat
shlep	drag
shlekht	bad, evil
tsores	problems
Shabbes	Sabbath
shvartza yor	black year
shidukh	marriage match
shadkhen	match maker
shtetl	village
shoin	already
shtik	play
swovo hanoro	I promise
shvayg	shut up
tatashi	daddy
tukh	scarf
trern	tears
Varsheh	Warsaw
vay iz mir	the pain is upon me
vayb	wife
veg	way
ver	who
wilkomen	welcome
yau	yes
yeshiva bokher	religious student
Yid	Jew
zakh	thing
zog	say it
zun	son
zayt	see

THE DEAD MAN

INTRODUCTION TO *THE DEAD MAN*

In *The Dead Man*, Asch depicts a community near death, starving, dressed in rags, living among the rubble. He portrays a moment in history when the suffering of humanity is so widespread that the door between this world and the next is left wide open, as people die en masse. A soldier massacred on the battlefield steals back into the land of the barely living to try and reclaim something of his lost life—to bring his fiancée back to the cemetery with him.

In the opening scene, a woman demented by war and draped with the slogans of revolution in multiple languages ascends to the pulpit. She addresses the prostrate crowd of exhausted and injured refugees in a roofless synagogue nearly reduced to rubble, keening about the wretched state of the world, led by lunatics and abandoned by God. Reb Khonen, a once-prosperous community leader, throws her out of the synagogue and starts imploring the survivors to rebuild.

An intense discussion ensues in which the people decide if they should limit protection to only those they know or take in new refugees. What should they rebuild first—their homes, the synagogue, a shelter, or a hospital? Should they try to get in touch with America for support to rebuild or help with emigrating? Two unknown soldiers arrive and reveal that the British have said they would give Palestine to the Jews. It's a miracle. The community, led by Reb Khonen, will rebuild the synagogue first. To celebrate, they decide to have a wedding. Reb Khonen offers to marry his daughter Dina to a teenager who was too young to join the army.

His daughter refuses. She believes her dead fiancé, Yosef, is still alive, despite reports of his death. At that moment her fiancé, dressed in an army uniform, limps into the synagogue, weak and injured, surprising everyone that he is still alive.

In act two, Yosef visits his old, blind mother in her war-torn kitchen, where she lies by the stove on a straw mattress. She feels something is very wrong with her son. Yosef announces he has discovered a land where Jews won't be persecuted, with plenty of food and jobs for everyone. He describes what he has witnessed there. He tells Reb Khonen he wants to bring Dina to his new home. He tells his mother her childhood friends will be there. People who want to go to the new land should meet him that night at the crossroads not far from town. Suddenly the crowd erupts with the news that old Reb Nehemiah has collapsed in the synagogue and is near death. Children have also died.

Act three begins at dusk. Yosef leads his mother to the crossroads and encourages her to walk through. She does, disappearing into the darkness. Yosef sits on a rock nearby as a merchant appears, and Yosef shows him the way. Old Reb Nehemiah arrives, and he joyfully walks across, followed by a widow and her children and then three very hungry boys, who see the Messiah riding on a white horse and banquets of food. They feel like they are flying through the clouds. Finally Dina shows up. Yosef leads her under a black wedding canopy, but she is frightened. The voices of the community become increasingly louder, and the scene shifts to Yosef's home, where the women are standing vigil by Dina's sickbed. She is getting better. Reb Khonen turns to Yosef and drives him out. He slowly limps off.

The play is set in a border community devastated by war. Asch grew up in Kutno, a small town close to the Prussian border. As a child, he witnessed its streets filling with refugees escaping pogroms. They arrived in droves with tin teapots tied to their sacks, hoping to steal across the German border en route to America.[1]

During World War I, Asch traveled across America twice to raise money for the suffering Jewish communities of Europe. He joined the American Joint Distribution Committee and smuggled aid into Poland. After the war he visited the decimated communities throughout Eastern Europe, interviewed the survivors, and was particularly moved by the Jews in Kovno, who had suffered so greatly. Their first priority was to rebuild the synagogue and find a teacher for the children, even before they worried about their own homes.

In his testimony describing what he saw among the Lithuanian Jewish communities of 1919, Asch says: "Hundreds of thousands had to leave their homes within 25 hours. They had lived there hundreds of years, in one day and one night they were uprooted, not only the healthy, but the sick. The beds have to be carried out of the hospital with their sick occupants and when they died they had to be left on the road without burial . . . Thousands have perished of hunger, cold, and disease. Those that got back found their property destroyed, stores entered, homes devastated. In the interval between the departure of the Russians and the arrival of the Germans, the local Christian population took advantage of the Jews and carried away all of their property. Even furniture, bedding, doors, and windows were stolen. Wooden houses were taken apart and carted off. Homes were practically erased.

"The hunger in Kovno was indescribable, and I am talking of only a few weeks ago, when I was there to see it. The fear of pogroms, which has made the population panicky throughout the whole section, has made commerce impossible."[2]

When he returned to America, Asch advocated for the US government to create a channel for Lithuanian Jews to communicate with their relatives in America. He called upon Americans to help build hospitals and schools overseas, to send supplies and tools so the people could begin to work again. All of this is reflected in *The Dead Man*'s opening scene.

Although Asch remained as proud of his aid work as he was of his literary accomplishments, he found it so taxing and disturbing that he had a nervous collapse shortly after returning to America. He was forced to recuperate over several months. *The Dead Man* is Asch's re-creation of what he saw in Eastern Europe after the war.

In the play, Reb Khonen, like Lazer in *Our Faith* and Yankl in *god of vengeance*, wants to marry off his daughter, without consulting her, to someone she is not interested in. The war has only just ended, and no one even has a home with a roof. Marriage holds a prominent place in the continuation of Jewish communities, however. Many married after surviving horrendous circumstances. The Yiddish poet H. Leivick wrote a play about a wedding he witnessed on the grounds of the Fernwald death camp in 1946. In Act Three of *The Dead Man*, the wedding ceremony Yosef arranges for his bride under a black canopy in the cemetery recalls the ghoulish nineteenth-century folk tradition of plague weddings held in a cemetery as a way to ward off the cholera epidemic.

Reb Khonen reveals himself in the first scene as wanting to limit the people the community takes in. There are no gentile characters

---

1 Schalom Asch, "Rückblick," Jahrbuch (Berlin: Paul Zsolnay Verlag, 1931) (*Looking Back* trans. by Beate Hein Bennett).

2 "Says Jews starve in parts of Russia: Yiddish writer tells of finding dire destitution, especially in Lithuania," *New York Times*, June 25, 1919, p. 8.

in this play. He is referring to displaced Jews from other countries. His suspicions about others and concern for his daughter leads him to the truth about Yosef, and thus he is able to save his daughter from death.

Throughout the play the chorus of women gently mock the men who think they know the answers to this chaotic time. When a woman tries to speak from the *bima* at the top of the play, she is kicked out and called a lunatic. She is only telling the truth. Other women are told to shut up. While the men pontificate, the women get down to business, making the food, nursing the sick. Moreover, they are the first to realize the soldier is dead.

The Polish Jewish director Abraham Teitelbaum (1889–1947) staged and starred in the world premiere production of *The Dead Man* in January 1922. Though only thirty-three, Teitelbaum had worked in Yiddish theater the world over, including Poland, Russia, England, France, and Argentina, before he arrived in Chicago in 1919 to direct for the Chicago Dramatic Society. The up-and-coming Hollywood screenwriter Ben Hecht (1893–1964), then a columnist at the *Chicago Daily News*, raved about the play's opening at the thousand-seat Glickman's Palace Theater:

He stands between *Hamlet* and *Peer Gynt*, the strangely motionless one who has thrown the Westside into an uproar. There is no drama around him. He is a dead young man in uniform walking slowly, limply through the acts. This is all one remembers—that his eyes were open and unseeing, that his arms hung like a scarecrow's and that the fingers of his hands were curled in and motionless . . .

One comes out of the theater with a strange sense of understanding. The dead have spoken to one. It is never to be forgotten. The youth that was ripped to pieces in the trenches reached out his limp arms across a row of Westside foot lights and left a crying echo in one's heart: "My unlived days! My uneaten bread! My uncounted years! They lie in a little corner waiting and no one comes to them." You will see the play, perhaps, or you will wait until it is translated some day. But this month, the Westside is aglow with the genius of Sholom Ash and with the interpretive genius of Abraham Teitelbaum, who plays the dead man in uniform and who directed the production. I know of no performance today that rivals his.[3]

Ben Hecht and Sholem Asch stayed in contact. Hecht would later quote *The Dead Man* in his 1939 screenplay for *Wuthering Heights*. Nelly tells Lockwood in the movie that the voice he hears is Cathy, "sobbing for her unlived days and uneaten bread," which is not a quote from the original novel.

In another famous Yiddish ghost play, *The Dybbuk*, a young bride asks while visiting her mother's grave, "What happens to the unlived joys and pains, the unspoken prayers, words and thoughts of a person who dies too young?" Asch responds in *The Dead Man* that all those unlived days gather dust in the corners of the world, becoming a source of eternal anguish for the person whose life is brutally cut short.

In the same year as Teitelbaum's Chicago production, in 1922 Maurice Schwartz staged *The Dead Man* in New York starring himself as the dead soldier, Yosef, with Celia Adler as his fiancée, Dina. As usual, Schwartz directed the show for his Yiddish Art Theater. The premiere of Schwartz's production celebrated Asch's twenty years as a writer in tandem with the publication of a twelve-volume set of Asch's collected works. The intermission included

---

3 Hecht, Ben, *"Dead Warrior,"* *A Thousand and One Afternoons in Chicago*, a public domain book, 1922, pp. 166–168.

spoken tributes to Asch's talent by *Forverts* editor Abe Cahan, writers Yehoash (1872–1927) and Shmuel Niger (1883–1955), and the poet Avrom Reisen (1876–1953), who once lived in a dingy carpenter's workshop with Asch when they were both penniless writers in Warsaw at the dawn of the twentieth century.

In 2003, Aaron Beall directed my one-act English language adaptation of Asch's *The Dead Man* with a cast of twenty at the Eldridge Street Synagogue on New York City's Lower East Side. The synagogue had yet to be renovated, and we placed the actors amidst the audience and on the bima. Dina called down from the women's balcony to her fiancé Yosef, who limped in from the back of the shul. Inspired by my time with Luba Kadison, studying the theatrical techniques of the Vilna Troupe, we painted the faces of the actors in white with exaggerated black eyes. Everyone wore rags. Only Yosef, the dead man, was makeup free. In 2021 Lisa Newman commissioned me to record *The Dead Man* as a radio play for the Yiddish Book Center, which we did during the coronavirus pandemic. As a safety precaution, we recorded each of the twenty-seven actors one by one and edited them all together with the assistance of the Yiddish radio artist Shahar Fineberg. Sholem Asch's great-grandson David Mazower introduced the play. That production debuted on April 25, 2021, during a sold-out Zoom event as part of Carnegie Hall's Voices of Hope Festival and is available for on-demand listening on the Yiddish Book Center's website.

Perhaps with the passage of nearly a hundred years we can finally bear to look at what Asch saw when he visited the Jewish communities of Eastern Europe after World War I, because for all its poetry, *The Dead Man* reveals a horrific scene of man's inhumanity to man.

The play is a meditation on the brutal injustices of war, painting a picture of multigenerational damage, serving as a reminder of what we as humanity are to avoid at all costs. There is no plot reveal. We know from the play's title that the soldier is dead and from the play's opening scene that the townspeople are barely alive. The audience only watches because they can't look away. They bear witness to an interpretation of the art that Asch created after he bore witness to suffering so horrific that it led to a nervous breakdown.

While Asch cannot give his dead soldier a life, he forces us to gaze at his absence of one. He wants us to be as haunted as he was looking directly into the face of what was lost. To remember, as Ben Hecht points out, the soldier's blank gaze, crooked hand, and sloping walk, trying to hold on to the thinnest thread of a life, we the living take for granted at our peril by ignoring what comes on the other side. Unlike the endings of Asch's dramas *On the Road to Zion* and *A String of Pearls*, this time there is no messianic shofar blown to alter life's circumstances. Once the soldier departs, those left alive must come up with their own solutions. And yet by banishing *The Dead Man* to the afterlife without his bride and allowing the community to rebuild, Asch allows for the possibility of new Jewish life in Poland, not imagining, and yet also foreshadowing, the future devastation that was to come.

ORIGINAL CAST

Introduction	David Mazower
Announcer	Shay Saul Guttman
A Madwoman	Caraid O'Brien
Reb Khonen, *a community leader*	Hal Robinson
Dina, *his daughter, 18*	Caraid O'Brien
Reb Nehemiah, *an elderly Jew*	Shane Baker
Reb Barukh-Leybush, *a local man*	Mark Greenfield
Reb Chaim, *a once-prosperous man*	Timothy Tanner
The First Foreigner	Corey Carthew
The Second Foreigner	Shahar Fineberg
The First Jew	Laura Zambrano
The Second Jew	Corey Carthew
The Third Jew	Mark Greenfield
The First Woman	Rachel Botchan
The Second Woman	Andrea Darriau
The Third Woman	Vered Hankin
The Abandoned Wife	Tara Bahna-James
The Widow, Brakha	Rachel Botchan
The Widow's children, *ages 3, 6, 9*	Miriam Tanner, Nicholas Tanner, Oliver Tanner
The First Merchant	Shahar Fineberg
The Second Merchant	Corey Carthew
The Third Merchant	Mark Greenfield
The First Boy, Yosele, *age 14*	Mannix MacCumhail
The Second Boy, *age 13*	Elijah Bahna-Outman
The Third Boy, *age 12*	Jonah Kaufman
Yosef, *a soldier returning from the war*	Aaron Beall
Mother, *Yosef's widowed mother*	Laura Simms
Villagers	Sally Atkinson, Lisa Newman
Angels Singing	Kate O'Brien, Cordelia James

CAST

A Madwoman

Reb Khonen — a Jew in his 40s

Dina — his daughter, 18 years old

Reb Nehemiah — an older Jew

Reb Barukh-Leybush — a once-prosperous man

Reb Barukh-Leybush's young son

Reb Chaim — a once-prosperous man

The First Foreigner

The Second Foreigner — a tall young man

The First Jew

The Second Jew

The Third Jew

The First Woman

The Second Woman

The Third Woman

The Abandoned Wife — who does not know if her husband is dead or alive

The Widow, Brakha

The Widow's two children — a boy and a girl

The First Merchant

The Second Merchant

The Third Merchant

The First Boy, Yosele

The Second Boy

The Third Boy

Yosef — a soldier returning from the war

The Mother — Yosef's widowed mother

The Crowd — men, women, children, both local and foreign

A small town in Eastern Europe, somewhere near a border, 1919

The old world is sick
The patient longs for death
Fools hold on
Madmen lead the way

ACT ONE

People slump in the corners of a roofless synagogue, half reduced to rubble. A madwoman festooned with ribbons bearing different slogans wears a placard with a giant Star of David on one side and "Long Live the Revolution" written in Russian on the other side. She stands behind the lectern and addresses the prostrate shadows.

Madwoman   Oh, how did we all get here from the four corners of the world? Our world is a rat cage and someone torched the four corners of that cage and the rats scurried out from the fire. God ran up to heaven, slammed the door behind him. He was afraid that it would reach Him too. The old world is sick. The patient longs for death. Fools hold on. Madmen lead the way.

Reb Nehemiah   *(an elderly, humble Jew comes in, sees the madwoman on the altar and groans)* This is what I survived for? Lunatics living in the synagogue. *(he pulls out a few torn pages from his pocket)* There are no prayer books left. Good that people still remember a little by heart. *(mumbles prayers to himself)*

Reb Khonen   *(a tall Jew with a long beard and a drawn face enters, sees the madwoman)* And now this. A synagogue is no place for crazies. *(he expels the madwoman from the synagogue)* All kinds of people are wandering around the country now. Difficult to know who's from here, who's a foreigner.

Reb Nehemiah   What difference does it make? Everyone looks familiar. Everyone looks foreign. Do you know where you'll be tomorrow?

Reb Khonen	No, no, the synagogue is only for the locals. Our people are struggling to return home from other countries. Their houses are destroyed, they'll have to live in the synagogue for the time being. First, we need to worry about ourselves; then we can deal with the others. *(gesturing to the foreigners)* Why've they been dumped on us? They're flooding us like an ocean. We can barely cope with our own people. Every day, new people arrive. Where are we going to shelter them all?
Reb Nehemiah	It's no secret the world was destroyed. God sent us a storm, the entire town decimated, entire cities, wiped out across the entire country. People don't know who is here, who is there, who is alive, who is dead.
Reb Khonen	It has to stop. We have to put an end to this tragedy. We have to start living like human beings. A new beginning, a completely new beginning. We must start living again now. If we don't, nothing will ever change. *(a few people enter)* Oh, just look what they've turned the synagogue into? A poorhouse! A lunatic asylum! Before we do anything else, we must draw a line between foreigners and our own people. If we don't, nothing will ever happen. Then we have to put a roof on the synagogue. It's urgent that we begin to live anew. If not, nothing will ever happen. What do you say, Reb Barukh?
Reb Barukh-Leybush	First we have to rebuild the community. If we want to have a synagogue, we must have a community. Without people, without community, there is no synagogue.
Reb Chaim	And what about a Talmud Torah? First thing, we need to hire a teacher, a *melamed* for the children. What is a city without learning? When we have a school, only then will we have a city.
Reb Nehemiah	And I think also a small hospital. Our people are return-

ing from foreign lands. There are so many wounded, *Rakhmone Letslan*, God have mercy on us. I think we need a hospital.

Reb Khonen *(irritated)* And tell me what else does your heart desire? Perhaps also a nursing home? With Jews, it's always the same. We don't even have a homeless shelter, not even a roof over the synagogue, and he wants a hospital already. Keep your wants to yourself until later.

Reb Nehemiah I only meant that with so many sick people, God have mercy.

Reb Khonen Before we do anything else, what about this shelter? I'll give a wall from my house. In any case, my home has been destroyed. The goyim pulled it down when we weren't there. Reb Barukh, how much will you give? You usually give something.

Reb Barukh *(staring at him)* From what's left of my estate?

Reb Khonen We give what we have. It is crucial that we figure out how to live like we did before.

Reb Barukh *(groaning)* Take the roof from my house to cover the synagogue. It's better my house is without a roof than the synagogue.

Reh Khonen See, we already have a roof for the synagogue and a wall for the shelter. Who else can give something? Reb Chaim, why aren't you saying anything?

Reb Chaim Take the window and the door from my house—I've nothing left to steal, and winter is still far enough away.

Reb Khonen *(pleased)* Jews, look, we are rebuilding our town. We are rebuilding our town, *o va!*

Reb Nehemiah	Wait. I think we need to hold off on rebuilding the synagogue until our neighbors return from the war. It's not right for us to snap up all the mitzvahs and do all the good deeds ourselves.
Reb Khonen	There'll be plenty left for them to do.
The First Jew	You should write to America. I was in Lakhmanov. The Jews there receive a ton of support from America, sacks of money.
The Second Jew	That's what they say. What are you building, a shelter, a synagogue? Write to America and you'll soon have a shelter, a shul—you'll have bread, whatever you want, you'll have.
The Third Jew	You can say that again. If only we knew the way to America, then we wouldn't need to worry. If America only knew of our troubles. *(hearing the word "America," everyone starts coming together)*
The Crowd	Who's talking about America? What's this about America?
The First Jew	My oldest son is there.
The Second Jew	*(holding out a piece of paper with an address)* My uncle, my mother's brother.
The Third Jew	So what! An uncle. My own brother's there!
The Second Woman	What are you talking about? America, my husband's there, my husband!
The Crowd	Take this address. I am begging you, take this address. Here, you have the address. *(everyone from all sides starts handing Reb Khonen pieces of paper with addresses on them)*

Reb Khonen	Everyone calm down. We have not found the way to America yet. *(they quiet down)*
The First Woman	Such smart Jews. They're so much smarter than everyone else, building a synagogue, a shelter. If only they knew the way to America.
Reb Khonen	We're cut off from the world. We're all alone. War on all sides. Death lays in wait on every journey. We don't know who we belong to; today we're one country, tomorrow another. We have no one to go to. No one is paying attention to us.
The First Woman	Then why are you still speaking about America? Shut up already about America. Better to say nothing.
The Second Woman	Why do you have to pour salt on our wounds?
The Third Jew	*Akh*, America, *Amerike!* If I could only will it so that this little piece of paper *(he holds up the paper with an address on it)* would take me there, to my brother's son. We called him Leybush at home. I lent him his first 25 bills when he was traveling to America, if he knew what kind of situation I was in! *Sha*, or even go to my brother-in-law, my wife's brother. In Brooklyn, he lives, near New York. At home we use to call him Chaim the wig maker. Akh, *Gotenyu, Tatenyu!* If I could just write him a letter, I would win everyone over, you know, as I live and breathe, as you see me standing here alive.
The First Jew	We're more connected to America than you are. We've very close relatives in America. A nephew, a brother-in-law. So what, a nephew! So what, a brother-in-law! My own son is in America, do you understand? *(pushes the address in his face)* Right here are the addresses.
The Second Woman	Give me a break, so it's their America already. My own hus-

	band lives there. The father of my children. And it's their America. A pox on all their houses, they don't know what they're talking about! It's their America!
Reb Khonen	Don't argue, don't argue, there's enough of America for all of you. America is big enough. Let's first figure out how to get to America.
The Third Woman	I just want to know one thing. Are they thinking about us at all? Do they even care?
The Second Woman	What's the difference if they can't help us?
Reb Khonen	*Sha*, don't say that, every day new Jews are arriving. Maybe we can find out more from them. *(More Jews enter, carrying bundles on their backs. Reb Khonen looks at them.)* Locals? *Sholem aleichem.* Welcome.
The First Foreigner	We're on our way back to our village.
Reb Khonen	Where are you coming from?
The First Foreigner	We come from the other side, where it was once Russia.
Reb Khonen	And what's there now?
The First Foreigner	Chaos and emptiness, the way it was before God created the world.
The Second Foreigner	*(tall young man)* No, it's like the time of the flood.
Reb Khonen	What are you saying?
The First Foreigner	It's an abandoned world. Whoever wants, whoever can, comes and takes.

The Second Foreigner	There's no law and there's no judge.
Reb Khonen	God's punishment for Cain's sin, after so many years of bloodshed, after blaspheming God. The clouds gather long before the storm crashes down. And of our brothers, the sons of Israel, what news do you have?

The younger man groans.

The Crowd	What? *Vos?*
The First Foreigner	Jewish blood flows down the streets like a river.
The Second Foreigner	It's like the destruction of Jerusalem.
The First Foreigner	With fire and sword, the enemy annihilates us. Whoever escapes the sword, perishes in the fire.
The Second Foreigner	And whoever escapes the fire succumbs to plagues and epidemics.
The First Foreigner	We've been erased from the face of the earth.
The Crowd	*(crying out)* *Oy vey iz undz.* The pain. Oh, our pain!
The First Jew	*(to Reb Khonen)* Why is this happening to us? Why does God beat us for a stranger's sin?
Reb Khonen	We see only our suffering because we are in pain. Can't you see God's hand in there? We have begged him day and night to show us his righteousness and erase the evil empires from the face of the earth with a burning hand. Today it's happening, we're the miracle before our own eyes. God decimated a strong and powerful enemy, and we're not happy about it because it upsets our own lives.
The Third Woman	*(angrily to Reb Khonen)* He punishes the goy, but He hurts us

too. He pours out grief and hate on us. On us! Look, look what he has turned us into.

Reb Khonen Who are we exactly that because of us, God should not enact his righteousness? And even if it affects our lives—we should be joyful. He punishes only our body, but He annihilates their soul. May they be wiped off the face of the earth. Do you understand? Do you get it?

Reb Nehemiah *(to the foreigners)* What are people saying where you're from? What do they think it all means? Why do they think this happened? How will it end?

The First Foreigner You haven't heard anything? *(the two foreigners stare at them)* They say that everything is because of the Jewish plot to push out the Turks.

Reb Khonen Are you listening to this? Do you hear this?

Reb Nehemiah Tell us, Jews, tell us, we're cut off from the world.

The Second Jew Without a newspaper, without even a letter—we don't know what's happening in the world.

Reb Khonen No one comes to tell us anything. For how long will it be like this and for what? And when will it end?

The Crowd Tell us, please, God, tell us.

The First Foreigner The governments sit in Paris and think up plans and write laws so that there should be no more wars in the world.

The Second Foreigner But it's all still meaningless.

Reb Khonen What do you mean? Is there no justice left in this world?

The First Foreigner	They'll give the land of *Yisroel* to the Jewish nation forever to compensate for all of our suffering.
The Crowd	*(shouting)* What? *Vos?*
The First Foreigner	The English king made a solemn promise.
The Second Foreigner	The English are useless. The Americans, that's who can do it. Only the Americans have the power to give it away in black and white.
The Crowd	When was this?
The First Foreigner	Just now.
The Second Foreigner	Jews are traveling there already. First Odessa, on small boats. Jews afloat on the Black Sea.
The First Foreigner	We're still waiting for them to open the border. The whole place is unprotected, everything we own is still there. After that, we'll go to *Yisroel*.
The Second Foreigner	That's a fact. That's a fact.
The Third Jew	How do you know all this?
The First Foreigner	You know how we know? The world is ringing with it. It's in all of the newspapers.
The Second Foreigner	We're just waiting until they open the border. America will send us ships with our own sailors who speak the holy tongue, Hebrew, and all aboard we go, to the Land of Israel, no less.
The First Woman	And what's the story with the food?

The Widow	And with milk?
Reb Nehemiah	And with medicine for the sick?
The Second Foreigner	Everything's been taken care of. Everything. Clothes and food. It's all ready on the other side waiting for us. Everything. We just have to wait until it's safe to bring it over the border.
The First Foreigner	And for everyone, there's a house and some land already, horses and tools, everything that you could need.
The Second Foreigner	It's all done in a very profitable way, like only the Americans can.
The Third Jew	*Gotenyu, Gotenyu,* what more do I need then? A house to live in, a little piece of land for grain, a little garden for vegetables in the summertime, a cow for milk for the grand-children, a horse and wagon, a pair of oxen and little lambs, just like it was in Biblical times. What more do I need?
The Crowd	*(gathering around)* Of course! *Avade! Azoi!* Sounds good! Can you imagine?
Reb Khonen	*(to the Jews gathered around him)* I've always said there is a reason for everything. A world doesn't go crazy for nothing. You don't kill off a world full of people, turning countries into ruin, for nothing. There must be a meaning behind it, a purpose for it. Now, Jews, do you understand the reason why?
The Third Woman	I am afraid to speak up, but I don't understand. Please don't kill me, you are smart people. But you know, on one side, they are saying that people are killing off all of the Jews. Jewish blood runs like rivers in the streets. But on the other side such incredible salvation and comfort prepared for the Jews. It's enough to make you crazy. But I'm just a foolish housewife.

Reb Khonen	Let me explain it to you. First of all, before the Messiah comes, there will be the absence of the Messiah, yes? Terrible times will reign all over the world. Every soul will tremble in its body like sand through a sieve.
Reb Nehemiah	*(nodding his head)* Just as it's written in our Holy Books.
The Crowd	*(to the foreigners)* When is this going to happen? When? When?
The Second Jew	We don't have any more strength to wait. No strength.
The Widow	Our children are dying before our eyes.
The Second Woman	And so are we!
The First Foreigner	It'll still take a little more time.
The Second Foreigner	Until everything is in order.
Reb Khonen	*(joyfully)* There is a God in this world. This is justice, righteousness. No, no. We have to start living anew. We have to live and we will live. There'll be an end soon to all of this horror. We must forget what was. The dead are dead. We can't bring them back from the dead as God ordained it. But the living need to live. Righteousness and justice will be established in this world. No more running, no more panic. Mine will be mine and yours will be yours. Our neighbors will return with God's help. But we all need to get back to business. We'll build up our town once again. We will live to see this happen. With God's help, this will all come true. Haven't you been listening to what these foreign Jews have been telling us? What governments of the world will undertake for us? We're to have our own land! A Jewish state! What do you mean that the world is ruined? We only have to start living again.

The Crowd	But how? How?
Reb Khonen	Look, I'll show you how! I've only one daughter. I found a groom for her, a fine young man. I loved him like my own son, but he was killed in the war. Now, if it's the will of God, I'll make my daughter a bride once again. Today! I'll take Barukh-Leybush's young son. People say that he's still too young, but we can't wait for him to get older. This is a time of chaos. And even though we have nothing, both our families are poor now, but I'll give the new couple a piece of my remaining estate so that they should live like all Jews live in this present time. *(he brings over Reb Barukh-Leybush's son)* And I'll commit myself to giving him several gold coins as a dowry as soon as God helps me to earn a living once again. In honor of our two esteemed guests who brought us such happy news, today following afternoon prayer, we will write the marriage contract. It'll be the start of a new time. We don't have any honey cake or brandy. Instead, we have each other, decent, venerable people, a shul full of Jews, no evil eye. And maybe, when we are all together, we can find a small piece of bread to make a blessing. *Yau?*
The Crowd	It's a good sign.
Reb Nehemiah	The first wedding contract in the new shul!
The Third Woman	To scare off the Angel of Death.
The First Foreigner	To begin a new life.
Reb Barukh-Leybush	I'm ready, my wares are ready, and I think this makes a lot of sense. But is it wrong to do it so suddenly?
Reb Khonen	I've wanted to ask you for a while. But despite my best efforts, time flew by. There's no reason to wait for the right clothes, all said and done, we don't have any, you know.

184

Same with the dowry. If you want me to, I'll sign something. Just as I said to you, even though it's unofficial. My door and windows, the goyim dragged off. My remaining wall, I promised for the shelter. They'll live like we live, how we have to live. Just as we all will live, for right now, until God gives us better times.

Reb Barukh-Leybush   If it works for you, it works for me. As I said, maybe this is the best way. May our children have better luck than us and bring good fortune to all the Jews.

Reb Khonen   That's just what I mean.

Reb Nehemiah   It's the old Jewish way.

Reb Khonen   It occurred to me the moment those Jews told us the good news heard around the world. I'll go get my daughter, and you, Reb Barukh, go see if there's a Jew here who can write the holy script. Maybe there's a scribe here among the foreign Jews?

The Third Jew   And don't worry about the food. There's enough Jews around here that sleep on sacks of money.

The Second Jew   And our government supplier has a full cellar of potatoes stored away. And bread up to his roof.

The First Jew   And there is no guard there, no policeman.

Reb Khonen   What's going on with you, Jews? Just out of chaos, out of danger, when finally the world begins to return to itself, and you want to go to prison? Don't worry, I still have enough for a meal for my daughter. Look, even in wartime, a Jew always puts something aside for these things. *(he unties a ribbon that he carries over his heart)* Take this money. Go out and buy whatever you can from the supplier. And tell the women

185

to prepare a meal for all the Jews who want to celebrate with me.

The Second Woman   (*excitedly*) We'll make a fire in the courtyard.

The Third Woman   Everything will be ready.

Reb Khonen   (*to his in-law*) You know, if our wives had only lived, it would have been different. When times are so wretched, you understand, a father has nothing to offer. Because of that you must take her as she is. The bride has no clothes, no jewelry. She will come to you as she walks and talks, nothing else.

Reb Barukh-Leybush   I understand. I understand, same as the groom. (*Reb Khonen goes off. A group of women go prepare the food. Other people prepare the marriage contract.*)

The First Women   (*going over to the others*) *Vey iz mir*, people are saying that her fiancé from before the war is still alive.

Women   Whose fiancé?

The First Woman   Reb Khonen's daughter.

The Second Woman   What are you saying? Aaron, the hatmaker's son, came home and told the story himself. The boy died in battle together with Pesie-Aytl's husband. He helped bury them himself in a Jewish cemetery in a Polish town.

The First Woman   But Nakhum-Leybush told everyone that people saw her fiancé in a Russian city, trading tea.

The Third Woman   And when Reb Chaim came back, he said that many of our people were captured by the Germans and are in Germany.

The First Woman   (*who has come over to join the women*) No, they've already left Germany. I heard he was seen with my husband in Holland, they're saying, or somewhere. He was held prisoner there because he stole across the border.

The Second Woman Anyways, he was only a fiancé. What are the other wives supposed to do, the ones with children who don't know if their husbands are alive or dead?

She points to the abandoned wife, who starts to cry.

The First Woman *(consoling the crying woman)* You shouldn't believe that your husband's dead, like Reb Khonen's daughter's fiancé. He's with my husband, deep inside Russia. They've become rich. Trading sugar. A man that came from there, he told me himself.

The Second Woman Yes, yes, many of them are rich. They're just not able to write to us is all.

The Third Woman *(coming over and speaking to the weeping woman)* Don't believe what they're telling you. It's a lie. Beryl-Chaim said that they're dead. He helped bury them in a Polish town. You're an *aguna*, a widow but worse. With no proof he's dead, you've no chance of getting married again.

The Abandoned Wife Stop it, stop it. You're making me crazy. He is dead, he is alive. It's all the same to me. *(weeps)*

The Third Woman *Akh*, happy are the wives whose men are in America.

The First Woman First of all, they're not at all certain about those men either. *(murmurings)* They say that those husbands, with wives here at home, get married again to someone else over there, live in beautiful buildings, have children with their American women. Many years go by, they haven't seen their wives, so the American rabbis give them divorces—those are the laws in America.

The Second Woman	*(who has a husband in America)* That's a lie, a lie. Our husbands are waiting for us. Write to my husband, I'll send him my picture. *(takes out a letter)*
The First Woman	*(squabbling with them)* Sure, so they live like princes over there, rich in luxury and pleasure—you think they'll take their old wives back?
The Third Woman	My God, what are they saying? Stop it, stop it, or we'll all go crazy!

The women go back to preparing the food. Reb Khonen enters with Dina, 18 years old, poorly but modestly dressed, wearing well-worn clothes that were once fashionable. She is barefoot.

Reb Khonen	Why don't you want this marriage? You don't like the groom?
Dina	No. I think he's alive.
Reb Khonen	Who's alive?
Dina	Yosef.
Reb Khonen	Your first fiancé? What are you saying? You know Beryl saw him buried with his own eyes. You know Beryl was right there—Yosef died together with Pesie's husband. They both fell in battle.
Dina	No, Tata, no.
Reb Khonen	Beryl served with him in the same regiment. They were together the whole time. The rabbi himself gave witness to his death.
Dina	No, Tata. He is alive.

Reb Khonen	How do you know that?
Dina	He comes to me every night in a dream, stands beside me, so tall and thin and emaciated. He begs me in such a pleading voice, the same way he used to cry for me to wait for him. He will come back for me.
Reb Khonen	Nonsense. Living people do not appear in dreams. Face up to reality. Only dead people show up in dreams.

Suddenly a tall young man wearing a soldier's coat appears at the door. He is very thin and stiff. He carries an empty sack on his back and shuffles forward slowly with the aid of a stick. The women by the door notice him first and stare at him.

The First Woman	Who is that?
The First Jew	I just saw him go in.
The Third Woman	Look how slowly he walks. Just like a shadow.
The Second Woman	It's from weakness.
The First Woman	I feel like I know him. I'm afraid to say anything.
The Second Woman	What do you mean?
The First Woman	Look at him. He looks like—
The Second Woman	*(half shouting)* My God! What am I seeing?
The Third Woman	You don't recognize him? Look at him closely.
The Women	*(suddenly start shouting)* Reb Khonen, Reb Khonen, Reb Khonen!
Reb Khonen	*(from far away)* What is it? Who's calling me?

Reb Khonen comes face to face with the pale young man, stands there a moment, shivers, and then looks at him closely. From far off we hear Dina cry "Yosef! Yosef!" She wants to run to him but some instinct stops her. Her father holds her back with his hand. Yosef raises his eyes. He holds out his hand as if to greet people.

Reb Khonen *(not shaking his hand)* You know, people said—

Yosef *(with a weak voice)* What did they say?

Reb Khonen That you were dead. God forbid. Killed in battle.

The Widow *(trembling)* Killed together with my husband.

Yosef *(with a strange smile)* But if someone dies, does that mean he is also dead?

Everyone looks at him strangely

Reb Khonen I don't understand what you mean.

Reb Nehemiah What's not to understand. Didn't we all die? How many times did we look death in the face? How do you know that we are not dead?

Yosef nods his head.

The Crowd Of course, *avade*, so, *azoi*.

SLOW CURTAIN

ACT TWO

A large room with the door and windows gone. An old woman lies in one corner on a straw mattress in front of a wrecked fireplace. Dina sits beside her.

Dina　I always said to you, Mother-in-law, that he is alive. My heart told me but you didn't want to believe me.

The Mother　Where is he? Where is my child?

Dina　He's coming soon with my father. I came first to tell you. I didn't want you to get a shock. He looks awful.

Yosef appears where the door should be. He enters followed by Reb Khonen, Reb Nehemiah, men, women, and children. His mother sees Yosef from across the room and stretches out her hand to him.

The Mother　My child, my child, you came at the right time.

Yosef shuffles over to his mother

The Mother　Come, my child, hurry. Why do you walk so slowly, my child? *(He goes to her. She touches him with her old hands.)* I already wept for you and now you stand before me alive. God, God, I am so thankful to you for what I see with my own eyes. *(she clings to him as Yosef remains cold, holding back)* You came back, now I am going there. *(She buries her face in his chest. Yosef is silent.)* Why aren't you saying anything, my child? Why aren't you speaking to me? *(Yosef is still silent)*

The Mother　Speak to me, Yosef. I want to hear your voice. Why are you silent, why?

Yosef	*(with a thin, weak voice)* What should I say, Mother?
The Mother	Are you Yosef? My child?
Yosef	It is I, Mama.
The Mother	My eyes are going. I cannot see him. Tell me, Dina, what has changed in him? How does he look?
Dina	*(looking at him)* He looks like always only a little emaciated.
The Mother	Something has changed in him. I don't know what. *(touching him)* His body is different. His voice is different. Tell me, good people, what did they do to him? I am afraid for you, my child.
Yosef	*(smiling)* Why are you afraid for me, Mama?
The Mother	Something has changed in you. I don't know what. *(one of the women glances at the other women standing by the door)* A mother's heart knows. Something about him feels alive but something else does not.

The First Foreigner taps his brow to indicate he understands.

Reb Nehemiah	What are they doing to them over there if they come home like this, one like this and the other like this?
The First Foreigner	This is how they come home. One of them came home to us like that, and he only remembered the way to his own house. Stayed sitting, just like that.
The Second Foreigner	Sometimes, forgetting is best. Once, when a soldier came home to us, he could not forget. He screamed all day, all night. Suddenly just started to scream and couldn't stop.

Reb Khonen	Stop it! *Genug.* Some return healthy, and others return sick. That's because there was a war on, you know. *(he goes over to Yosef, takes him away from his mother, says to her)* He's tired. He's come a long way and is hungry, so. *(to Dina)* Go next door and see if you can get him something to eat. He must not feel well.
Yosef	I am not hungry. And I feel fine.
Reb Khonen	How long has it been since you last ate?
Yosef	In the land where I come from, no one is hungry like this.
Reb Khonen	In the land where you come from? Where have you been all this time?
Yosef	I have been in another land that lies on the other side—
Reb Khonen	Is it far from here?
Yosef	No, not far. Just right behind the town, by the woods, over the hill, on the other side of the border.
Reb Khonen	*(surprised)* There's a border? I never knew our town was on a border.
Reb Nehemiah	What's the big surprise? They took the world and divided it, cutting it into parts. Each one of them gets a little piece for themselves. Wherever you stand today, there's a border.
The Second Jew	And we sit here blocked off from everywhere. Do we even know what's happening in the world?
Reb Khonen	Our country has a new name already.
The Third Jew	With completely different laws even!

The Abandoned Wife Did you maybe run into my husband over there? They call him Barukh, and he has a birthmark over his right eye. He used to trade flax. They say he's become very rich.

Yosef No, I met no one like that.

The Widow What about mine? He was together with you in the war. You know, people said that you were both killed, God forbid. Where did you leave him?

Yosef *(pointing with his hand)* In the land on the other side.

The Widow *(screaming)* He's alive?

Yosef I have a message for you from him. He sent something with me.

The Widow But he's alive?

Yosef He was captured.

The Widow *(doesn't let him speak)* Why didn't he come here with you?

Yosef The border is blocked.

The Second Woman *(to the widow)* Don't believe him, Brakha, you're a widow. Your husband's dead.

The Second Jew *(to Yosef)* What about my son? He was with you in the same regiment.

The Third Jew What about mine?

Reb Khonen Let him be for a minute. *(to Yosef, trustingly)* And you, how did you get here?

194

Yosef	I stole across the border.
Reb Khonen	And why didn't we hear from you this whole time if you were still alive? You didn't send us a single message, no word, nothing.
Yosef	I did not have an opportunity.
The First Foreigner	There's no mail there?
The Second Foreigner	The borders are blocked in all countries. How could he have sent news?
Reb Nehemiah	What's happening in those other places? Are we fighting with the Russians or with the Germans?
Yosef	Neither. There, on the other side, we have already made peace.
The Crowd	*(calling out)* You hear? They made peace!
Reb Nehemiah	What? They're not fighting any more? What do you mean? How can that be?
Yosef	It is quiet there now.
The Crowd	Quiet there now. *Shtil.*
The Second Jew	And what have you heard over there about the food supply?
Yosef	It is no longer a crisis.
The First Woman	What? They get food there by you? Every day?
The Second Woman	What, no one's hungry in that land?

The Third Jew   *(to the others)* What's he saying?

Reb Nehemiah   What do you mean? People are getting enough food there?

Yosef   They are not in need of that.

The First Jew   How can that be?

Reb Nehemiah   Listen! You know, if people aren't in need of it, then it must be, you know—

The Widow   Is there milk for the children?

The First Boy   How about rolls with butter, can you get them there now? Like before the war? What about pastries filled with jam?

The Second Boy   *(pushing him away)* Are there cheesecakes and stuffed honey cakes with butter like my Mama used to give out on *Simchas Torah*—do they get that there also?

The First Merchant   *(pushing the kids away)* Who cares about food. What do you hear about jobs? Can you make a living over there?

Yosef   People are not worried about that.

Reb Nehemiah   What do you mean?

Yosef   Listen to me. Everyone has what they need there.

The Second Jew   What more do they need then?

The First Woman   And here we sit, unable to go anywhere, knowing that kind of country exists in the world.

The Second Woman   But didn't you hear? It's not so far from our town.

The Third Jew	*(pointing toward Yosef)* Answer me. Is that land far away from us or not?
Yosef	For some it is far, and for others near.
Reb Nehemiah	What do you mean?
Yosef	It depends on which path you take.
The Second Jew	You mean there's both a long way and a short way?
Yosef	Just like you say.
The First Jew	Then why are we sitting here waiting for death?
The First Woman	Such wise Jews, they can't even tell that our savior is right behind the door.
Reb Khonen	*(to Yosef)* Then why do you look so weak, thin, and emaciated, barely able to stand on your feet?
Yosef	It is from longing. They are all there on the other side, longing for you all.
The Widow	Of course, you can waste away from it, when your family is so far away.
The Third Jew	Tell me, I'm begging you. How do we find the way there from here?
Reb Khonen	Shh, let him rest, don't you see he's tired? Let him be with his mother. *(looks at Dina, to Yosef)* Praise God. You've come home. Who would have thought? Blessed be the living and the dead. *(looks at Dina)* The bride and groom haven't seen each other in such a long time. Of course, they've a lot to talk about. Come Jews, let's leave them alone.

Reb Khonen leads the men, women, and children out of the house. They speak among themselves. Yosef and Dina are alone. The Mother sleeps in a corner.

Dina *(taking Yosef's hand)* Dear Yosef, where have you been all this time?

Yosef I was so near to you, but I could not come and visit you.

Dina I missed you so much.

Yosef I knew that.

Dina *(smiling)* How did you know that, Yosef?

Yosef I heard you missing me from the other side. Every night as you lay down in bed, I heard each of your groans and each of your heavy sighs. I heard you call out to me, but I could not answer you. I wanted to but I could not.

Dina *(surprised)* How did you hear me? You were so far away.

Yosef In the other land, on the other side, everyone hears from far away. The wind carries all the voices to us there. The air is transparent and we can see you from down the hill.

Dina Why didn't you send us any news of you?

Yosef At first, you were all so far away. I thought that I would never reach you. You would always be here and I there. But sometimes we can see when you are coming closer to us. And then I saw you with my mother, and you were so close. I called out to you. I spoke to you and it seemed like you heard my voice.

Dina *(smiling)* How so? Were we standing in the same place?

Yosef   It just seemed like we were. Everyone who goes moves so quickly, you think you are in the same place.

Dina   I don't know what you mean.

Yosef   In the stillness, beneath us, we travel very fast, anywhere we want to go in the world. We do not see how and we do not know how. Over there, on the other side, in the other land, if we look at you, we see you. As if you had hitched galloping horses racing closer, closer to us.

Dina   *(laughing)* You're joking, darling Yosef.

Yosef   Did you feel how close you were getting to me?

Dina   Yes, it was just like that. Many times it felt like you were standing behind our door or knocking on our shutters. When you opened the door and came into the house, no one could see you except for me, and sometimes you visited at night and you stood by my bed and said something to me, and sometimes I heard you speak inside of me. I heard your voice, but I couldn't see you.

Yosef   That is when I was calling you from there, from the other side. I spoke to you. I did not know if you heard me or not.

Dina   But everyone here said that you were already dead. That you were gone and that you would never come back. But I didn't believe them. I knew that somewhere, you were alive, waiting for me.

Yosef   I lived my entire life again. I lived through every day again. Every day and every hour.

Dina   *(looks at him astonished)* Yosef, what do you mean?

Yosef There on the other side, in the other land, I could only relive the life I lived here. Not one new day, not one new hour, nothing else happened, only what I lived here.

Dina Didn't you meet anyone there? Is that place deserted?

Yosef There are many people there, but each one of them lives only for himself, locked in his own world. Over and over, you experience there what you once lived here. I remembered every kiss you gave me, every look in your eyes, and every touch of your hand, every quirk and every gesture. How you laughed and how you cried. I experienced it all again, every joy, every sorrow.

Dina And you didn't think about our future together at all?

Yosef I only thought about what was.

Dina Why do you only speak of what was? Why don't you speak of what will be? We're both still so young with so much ahead of us.

Yosef is silent.

Dina Why aren't you answering me, Yosef? Why don't you kiss me? You haven't kissed me since you've been home.

Yosef I should kiss you.

Dina Yes, like you did before.

Yosef kisses her on the forehead.

Dina *(frightened)* Why are your lips so cold? Your hand is like a block of ice. *(looks at him)* Why are you so pale? I don't know you anymore.

Yosef　It is from missing you, Dina. We are there on the other side and we all long for those we left behind. All day and all night, we long for you. The longing tortures us and makes us all look so terrible.

Dina　What do you mean by that—us all?

Yosef　Everyone who is on the other side.

Dina　Are there many people we know there?

Yosef　Many people from here, that you thought were dead, live there.

(pause)

Dina　Is it good there?

Yosef　Not good and not bad, just as it needs to be.

Dina　And where will we live, here or there?

Yosef　I came to get you. How could I have just stayed there when I knew how bad it was for you here?

Dina　You want to take me there?

Yosef　Go with me to the other land. I came from there to get you.

Dina　From everything that you've said, it's so far and so strange.

Yosef　It will soon become more and more known all over the world.

Dina　Will my father come with us?

Yosef He still has time.

Dina What will it be like for us there, alone without family, without friends?

Yosef They will come, they will come. Everyone will go there eventually.

(pause)

Dina Is it difficult to cross the border?

Yosef The border is open on the way there. It is closed coming back.

Dina *(with longing)* So we must stay there forever? We can never come back?

Yosef That is how it will be.

Dina *(with longing)* Why must you go back? Stay with us.

Yosef I gave my word that I would return.

(pause)

Dina But where will we live there?

Yosef In our own house.

Dina Is it big?

Yosef No. Just for the two of us, alone.

Dina Where is it?

Yosef   In a little wood, on a hill, behind the town. The sun shines in summer, and in the winter it is covered with snow.

Dina   *(joyfully)* Oh, how beautiful.

Yosef   Do you want to see it?

Dina   We can see it from here?

Yosef   It is nearby.

Dina   Where?

Yosef points to the sky.

Dina   *(frightened)* In the sky?

Yosef   Look closely; you will see our little synagogue.

Dina   *(looking up into the sky)* Where? Where? I don't see anything, just clouds rolling, blue clouds spreading like thick dark veils encircling the moon.

Yosef   Over there, don't you see a wood? Thick with trees, one taller than the next, and beyond the treetops, a shining blue field. And do you see a hill there enveloped in blue shadows?

Dina   *(looking)* There by that blue streak? How do we even get there?

Yosef   You sail there on a little cloud.

Dina   *(listening closely)* Who is singing over there? I hear a song, a peaceful, quiet song.

Yosef   That is what they sing from the other land to here.

Dina   They're calling us.

Yosef   Over there in that direction.

Dina   *(startling, as if waking from sleep, frightened, looking around her)* What was that, Yosef? Where was I?

Yosef   Not far from here, not far.

Dina   You spoke so strangely, and I heard such a song. *(looks closely at Yosef)* I am afraid of you, Yosef.

Yosef   You were just dreaming. You were dozing off.

Dina   But it felt so good. I really want it to be like that, so why am I scared, Yosef?

Yosef   It is still so strange for you. You will get used to it.

Dina   Will it be like what we just saw?

Yosef   Of course.

Dina   Oh, how nice, only quiet, shhh, don't talk about it. It's our secret. *(quietly)* I am afraid of my father. He's so strict. In the end, he won't let me go with you.

Yosef   We will keep it a secret.

Dina   Good, Yosef. *(squeezes his hand)* Quiet. People are coming. *(moves away from him)* Shhh. Not a word.

The Widow   *(coming in)* I beg your forgiveness a thousand times over for disturbing you, but I couldn't restrain myself any longer.

Yosef said that he had a message for me from my husband. I've come to get my message. He left me alone with our two babies and no one knows where he is, if he's dead, if he's alive, one says he's dead, the other says he's alive.

Yosef He sent you a message that he bought his own plot of land.

The Widow *(joyfully)* Big?

Yosef Not big and not small, exactly as it needs to be.

The Widow And here we sit, dying for a little bite of food, and he lives there in his own home, abandoning us to trouble, poverty, and hardship.

Yosef He is always thinking about how to bring you and the children to him.

The Widow He's thinking about doing it? Yes?

Yosef Day and night. He cannot rest.

The Widow *(with a tear)* My poor husband, of course, that's just like him. How could life turn out well for him there when he knows what it's like for us left behind?

Yosef It gives him no rest.

The Widow And how's it working out for him there?

Yosef Not good and not bad. Just as it needs to be, whatever he needs, he has.

The Widow As we always say, what more do we need? Is he trying to figure out a plan?

Yosef That is his only concern.

The Widow And when will he take us there? How much longer?

Yosef At the first opportunity, at the first opportunity.

Reb Khonen *(enters with a few merchants)* Yosef, Yosef, come here, forgive us. *(Yosef goes to them)* These are decent people. *(points to the Jews)* Local merchants. They want to ask you some questions about business. *(to the Jews about Yosef)* My son-in-law has an eye . . .

The Merchants *(to Yosef) Sholem aleichem.*

Yosef *Aleichem sholem.*

The First Merchant *(to Yosef)* What are they dealing in over there, where you are, in that other place?

Yosef Everyone deals in whatever he traded at home.

The Second Merchant Is there someone there to buy nails from?

Yosef There are people who sell nails.

The Third Merchant And wool?

Yosef There are also wool merchants there.

The Second Merchant And ox and sheepskin?

Yosef There's no shortage of ox and sheepskin merchants either.

The First Merchant You can't gamble on a merchant! Are there honest people there we can trust? Could we get into business on the strength of our word?

Yosef	Yes, you do not have to worry about that, the most trustworthy people, big merchants, honest people, the most famous bankers in the world.
The First Merchant	Forget about merchants. What kind of money system do they use over there, rubles or marks, maybe kroner?
Yosef	They take all kinds of money there. People come to that place from every country and every state.
The Third Merchant	Money's useless. Can you make a living there?
Yosef	Every person has what they need.
The Merchants	What more do we need in these terrible times?
The Third Merchant	*(takes Yosef aside)* Young man, we could both become rich if we could buy sheep and oxen and bring them over here. It's a big business, tantamount to gold.
The Second Merchant	*(arguing)* But how could you bring them over? How could you cross the border?
The Third Merchant	That's what we're talking about, you know. We must figure out some scheme. Young man, we could become rich.
The Second Merchant	*(drags Yosef aside)* Who cares about oxen? Who cares about sheep! When we could bring over a wagon full of nails, or skeins of wool and linen.
The First Merchant	*(drags Yosef)* What's with the nails! What's with the wool! A penny trader. I have a sack stuffed full of bank notes, all types of rubles, tsarist rubles, Kerensky rubles, and Soviet rubles, German marks and kronen. I sleep on a straw mattress full of them. We can bring it all over to the other side. We can all become rich.

The Second Merchant	Why are we just sitting here?
The First Merchant	Why are we silent?
The Third Merchant	Why are we sleeping?
The Second Merchant	Let's take this young man and go over there.
Reb Khonen	We really need to think things over first, consider it deeply. *(they discuss amongst themselves)*
Reb Nehemiah	*(sneaks in and goes over to Yosef)* Forgive me, I wanted to ask you something.
Yosef	I am listening.
Reb Nehemiah	I'm an old man, full of troubles. I've endured too much in my life. I wandered all over this province. In these last years, what haven't I lived through? Who can remember it all? I'm tired. I want to rest my old bones. Is there anything in that land on the other side, where you came from, like a *bes medresh*, a study group, a shul, where old Jews sit, like in olden times, and study a page of *Gemorah*, a verse of the *Khumesh*, or say a few prayers? Somewhere we can find a few good pious Jews who could help out an old Jew with a bowl of soup, with a meal on Shabbos, once in a while a shirt for the bathhouse, like it used to be in the good old days.
Yosef	Old people sit in the study house and learn there day and night.
Reb Nehemiah	So! There are study houses over there!
Yosef	Yes, exactly. Only with more comfort, illuminated by a great, brilliant light, and old Jews from around the world with long white beards, covered in white *kittels* and *tallis,*

faces illuminated by the light of the holy *shekhina*, sitting around big wide tables, with big books of *Gemorah* opened wide. They learn by singing the old melodies.

Reb Nehemiah (*astonished*) *Azoi!* Jews are learning over there! Talmud scholars, *rabonim*, rabbis, heh?

Yosef Geniuses, *gaonim*, from all over the world, the greatest minds and the most venerated Jews.

Reb Nehemiah Shh—*azoi?* A wonder, never heard of it. Freed from the worries of making a living, *yau?* From all kinds of drudgery!

Yosef That is a small thing. Relieved of all worldly concerns. They live only spiritually.

Reb Nehemiah *Azoi!* Is it far from here? People say that border is difficult to cross, *yau?*

Yosef It is a well-worn path.

Reb Nehemiah So why are we sitting here, in poverty and in hardship, and for nothing. No time to think about anything other than how to get a little morsel of food. It takes away all our energy, with no time for other things, higher matters. Always burdened by the troubles of this world, trying to survive. If it is the will of God, soon after Shabbos, at the beginning of the week, I will take my stick and my sack and go on my way. I only ask that you'd be so kind as to show me the way.

Yosef It is not far, behind the town, on the hill, in the woods, you will see a trail.

Reb Nehemiah Right around here you mean? *Yau*, I understand.

Reb Khonen	*(standing the whole time, listening to their conversation at a remove, comes forward)* What are you talking about?
Reb Nehemiah	About a very important matter. *(to Yosef)* And we were just skimming the surface. Ah, thank you so much for the good news. *(goes off)*
Reb Khonen	*(to Yosef)* I understand some things, yes. But there's other things I don't understand. Usually I figure it all out pretty easily. Tell me, what do you plan to do?
Yosef	Go back there.
Reb Khonen	Is this a finalized matter?
Yosef	I have my place there, you know.
Reb Khonen	Let me be honest with you. Something seems strange to me, unknown, about all of this you've told us. I don't know if I can let my child go to such an unknown place in these troubled times.
Yosef	It is the only untroubled corner of the world.
Reb Khonen	Yes, that could be, but everything that you've explained, there's something so . . . I don't know what I'd have thought if I didn't know you or didn't know who you were. I'm not sure what I'd have thought about you. I won't say it again. In today's times, we hear about such bizarre things happening all over the world. God only knows what will be.
Yosef	Father-in-law, I think it is for the good. Here, everything is up in the air. The world trembles, agitated, we do not know what tomorrow will bring, chaos and plagues, hunger, and crisis. Death is better than that kind of life, you know.

Reb Khonen   That's true, but that's how it is now. People get used to it. From what you're telling us, everything's so unknown. Some things you say almost make sense, and then they seem distant, unknown, and strange. We don't know where you come from or what kind of country it is.

Yosef   Oh, it will become more and more known all over the world. People go there from all over. Everyone, running from hardship, finds peace there. And today because of the war, everyone goes to that place, young and old, women and children.

Reb Khonen   Yes, but no one has come back from there until now except for you.

Yosef   That is because the border was closed.

Reb Khonen   Could be. But since you spoke with Dina she's not been feeling well.

Yosef   Is she complaining about something? Is something causing her pain?

Reb Khonen   No, not that. She's saying such odd things, half gibberish, as if she was speaking from a dream or from a fever, God forbid.

Yosef is silent.

Reb Khonen   This whole situation bothers me; forget about that other place, put it out of your head. Stay with us. God will help us, we'll push through this horrible time.

Yosef   I cannot be here.

Reb Khonen   Why not? All kinds of Jews are here, why not you? Take a look, people are staying alive around here, thank God.

Yosef   I must go back to that place.

Reb Khonen   What place? Where?

Yosef   There, where I came from.

Reb Khonen   Why?

Yosef is silent

Reb Khonen   What? You gave your word? Promised? Or what?

Yosef is silent.

Reb Khonen   It must be something. Tell me. Why aren't you saying anything? Why? *(Yosef is silent)* Nu, you don't need to go back today. There's still time. We'll speak about it later. Meanwhile, let's say good night. Your mother is alone. Dina, come. *(Dina goes over to her father, quietly)* Something's off here, I can't quite figure it out. My daughter, come out of there, hurry up. *(Dina wobbles unsteadily on her feet)* What's wrong with you, Dina? Why have you gone so pale? Look, you can't even stand on your feet.

A woman runs for water. Reb Khonen looks at Yosef. Yosef is silent. A cry from outside. Everyone listens. A woman comes in.

The Third Woman   Reb Khonen, quick, old Reb Nehemiah fell in the shul.

Reb Khonen   He was just here.

The Abandoned Wife   *(coming in with a cry)* One of Soreh's little children just died!

Reb Khonen   *(grabs Dina and runs out with her)* Come quickly, time is of the essence. I won't let you go with him, my child.

Khonen runs off with Dina. The women run off distraught. Yosef and his mother remain alone. Yosef is quiet for a while, then slowly walks over to his mother and sits down by her mattress.

Yosef   Good evening, Mama.

The Mother   Who is there?

Yosef   It is I, your son.

The Mother   I've grown old and tired.

Yosef   I have come to take you home.

The Mother   Where's that, my child?

Yosef   Only one step over the threshold.

Mother   Will I have nice neighbors there?

Yosef   All of your old friends.

Mother   Who, my child?

Yosef   Your good friend Rokhl-Leah will be your neighbor to the right.

The Mother   Who? The Rokhl-Leah I spent my childhood playing with in the sand? We studied Hebrew with the same teacher. She went to America, you know. Her children came and brought her back with them.

Yosef   She's come back from America to us there.

The Mother   People are coming back to us from America too?

Yosef	From all over the world.
Mother	It must be a big place. And who else, my child?
Yosef	Khaya-Ratsa, who ran the little store in our town.
The Mother	The one who gave a whole pound of candles to the *bes medresh* every Friday?
Yosef	Yes, exactly.
The Mother	Is everyone there? I didn't know.
Yosef	She will be your neighbor.
The Mother	*(smiling good naturedly)* Where on earth?
Yosef	Over there. No, really, you will see.
The Mother	And how do they honor *Yiddishkayt* there, my child? Pray on Friday by the evening light, observe *Shabbos*? Do they honor the commandments of our people? People say that in those faraway places, children forget their *Yiddishkayt*.
Yosef	Soreh, Rivkeh, and Leah are the teachers in the women's shul.
The Mother	Who? Soreh, Rivkeh, Leah from the Bible? They are there with us?
Yosef	Along with many other pious women, holy mothers.
The Mother	*O va!* And Hanna with her seven sons?
Yosef	Lives with the Rebetsin on the same street as the *bes medresh*, not far from the shul.

The Mother	Do they go to shul?
Yosef	Every *Shabbos* in the morning.
The Mother	Will they let me pray in that shul?
Yosef	You already have a seat waiting there for you.
The Mother	If so, I have to take my silk dress with me, with the buttons, and my gold necklace. It's nothing compared to all those important people, all praying in the one shul! Yes, and my prayer book, put it with the Yiddish Bible, tie them up together. I can't forget my glasses. You'll carry my prayer book to the synagogue for me like you did when you were a little boy.
Yosef	Then you better give me a sweet bun with raisins.
The Mother	You remember that, my child?
Yosef	And I will pray with my father in the men's section.
Mother	And I will look down at you from the women's balcony.
Yosef	Just like it used to be.
Mother	Just like it used to be. *(pause)* We need to get ready to leave so that we're on time for shul. It's getting late. It's getting late.
Yosef	Give me your hand, Mama.
Mother	Where are you taking me, my child?
Yosef	On a journey, on a journey.

SLOW CURTAIN

ACT THREE

At a crossroads. From far away through an obscuring fog, we see a crumbling outpost. On either side of the road, bright clouds. A hill in the background. Dusk. Everything is covered in a dark sheen. Yosef enters with his mother.

His mother walks very slowly, dressed in her Sabbath dress with a new head scarf. Yosef walks after her, carrying her prayer book and her Yiddish Bible wrapped in a cloth.

Yosef   We have arrived at the border, Mama. You see the other town wall, that is the way. You have to go there alone. I need to wait here for other people.

The Mother   Where should I go, my child?

Yosef   Go right, Mama, to the other road. You will see a path straight into the shul.

The Mother   *(tries to go)* My eyes are so weak. I see nothing, my child.

Yosef   Put on your glasses. You know you need them to see, to read the Yiddish Bible and to pray with your *sidur*. Put them on, maybe then you will be able to see the path.

The Mother   Where did you put them, my child? Did I forget them at home?

Yosef   They're tucked inside the women's prayer book, folded up by the Prayer for the Dead.

The Mother   You are right, my child. O, what a bright road. Like a spring morning. And how it smells my child, like *Shavuos* in synagogue.

Yosef   That's the way, that's the way.

The Mother   And here's the shul already. Two women *gabbais* sitting on their bench, throwing spices out from their aprons.

Yosef   It's for you Mama, for you.

Mother   I will ask them for permission. *(she speaks as if she sees them)* Greetings, holy mothers, I, your servant girl, Devora, daughter of Leah, come knocking at the door of your holy shul. I want to pray with you in shul. I have my own prayer book. I brought my Yiddish Bible with me. And if you need me, I can say the blessing. I will stand by the door. I'm just a poor woman. Thank you so much. May God reward you for it. *(to Yosef from the road)* A *gut Shabbos*, my child, and when you meet your father, tell him that your mother went to shul to pray.

She disappears into the darkness. Pause. The first merchant with a sack on his back appears on the road.

The First Merchant   I packed my entire fortune into this sack, and I've come without the others. It's best to do business alone. I've several Russian rubles, from the time of the tsar only, not the modern paper money with the crown and signature. And today's German marks with the emperor's eagle, and genuine kronen, at least a thousand stamped and numbered. All in all, that should guarantee me passage across the border.

Yosef   You need to wait until the moon comes out from underneath the clouds.

The First Merchant   I understand with so much money, it's better to move in the dark. For now I'll sit on this stone counting my money to see if my total is correct. *(it grows dark)*

Yosef   There is no time. We need to get on our way.

The First Merchant   Where's the way?

Yosef   Over there, where you see the outpost.

The First Merchant   *(leaves alone)* It's so dark around here. I don't see any road. I don't see any path. *(turns back to Yosef)* But tell me, young man, is this the right way for certain? It won't be too dangerous to go by myself with so much money?

Yosef   Many merchants have gone there before on this same path.

The First Merchant   Is that right? *(groping himself)* Thank God, my money is everything I have. I feel it on my body. Now tell me, young man, is there no guard here to accompany me on the road, with a lantern, with a bit of light? I'll pay.

Yosef   Jingle your pocket so that people can hear you. *(the merchant does that)*

The First Merchant   Oh, people are coming toward me. Now I'm on the right path. Coachmen are driving merchants with their stalls. So much merchandise, the wheels are buckling. And look at the oxen, look at the sheep that people are bringing into the city. It must be a great city, a metropolis. And what do you know, the annual market is today, the Autumnal Fair! See those carriages filled with animal skins! And the spinning wheel with the woolen shawls and scarves. Look at the horses, look at the sheep! Big business here. My money is good. If it's the will of God, make me a living, put food in my mouth, in my mouth.

He disappears through the outpost.

The widow, letter in hand, arrives with her two children.

The Widow   My husband wrote me a letter. He said to come over to him with my children. I don't know the way myself. Will you show me the way?

Yosef   Right there on the path, through the outpost.

Widow   There, where it's so dark?

Yosef   You will find a way.

The widow and her children go onto the path.

The Widow   The road is dark. We don't see any light. Never mind me. God forbid, nothing should happen to the children. *(she pulls the children to her)* Hold on to my dress, don't get lost in the dark.

The Children   *(joyfully)* Mama, Mama, I see the light far away!

The Widow   Where? Where? It's dark everywhere.

The Girl   There, Mama, out of the darkness, a light shines and beams at us.

The Boy   We can see it from here. It lights the way.

The Girl   Like a lantern shining its light into the darkness straight at us.

The Widow   I don't see anything, only darkness around me, darkness everywhere.

The Children   Come with us, come with us.

They lead their mother by the hand.

The Girl   *(joyously)* Now I see a window, an open window with a lamp shining down on our path.

The Boy   Look, look who's sitting by the window and looking out at us.

The Girl   It's a man with a round black beard. He sits by the window and holds his head in his hand.

The Boy   He's looking straight at us.

The Girl   *(joyfully)* It's my Tata! Mama! I recognize him. He sits by the window and waits for us.

The Widow   Where? Where?

The Children   There, there! Right where the light is coming from!

They all disappear into the darkness.

Yosef   *(sitting this whole time alone on a stone, to himself)* Everyone, everyone, is coming, only she is left, so I sit here by the crossroads of death and life and wait and wait.

Reb Nehemiah enters with his pack on his back and a stick in his hand.

Yosef   Did you see my fiancée on the road?

Reb Nehemiah   Who? Reb Khonen's daughter Dina, the daughter of Malkale?

Yosef   Exactly, yes.

Reb Nehemiah   She's coming, she's coming. *(pause)* Still far to the city?

Yosef	Not far.
Reb Nehemiah	I didn't know this path was so popular.
Yosef	Were you here before?
Reb Nehemiah	More than once; almost made it to the border.
Yosef	You know you have to go alone?
Reb Nehemiah	With God's help, I will find the road. Then, first thing, I'll walk into the best, top study house and I'll stand by the door! I won't, God forbid, get lost among so many Jews, no evil eye. *Barukh hashem*, I will find a Jew that would like to do a *mistve* and bring a guest home. Why should I worry? *Nu,* good luck, it's getting late.

Reb Nehemiah shakes Yosef's hand and goes over to the outpost until he disappears behind the clouds.

Yosef	*(looking after him)* Good for him. Good for him.

Three boys enter.

The Boys	*(to Yosef)* Take us with you, take us with you.
Yosef	To where?
The Boys	Over to that place where you come from.
Yosef	It's still too early, still too soon.
The First Boy	I'm hungry here, there's food there.
The Second Boy	It's bad here, it's good there.

All Three	*(pleading)* Take us with you, take us with you.
The First Boy	We'll grab on to the back of a cart.
The Second Boy	We'll sit on the wagon shaft.
The Third Boy	We'll curl ourselves up in a ball and not take anyone's spot.
All Three	*(pleading)* Take us with you, take us with you.
Yosef	Will you be very quiet?
The Boys	No one'll hear us, no one'll see us.
Yosef	Steal across the border over there. When you get to the outpost, you're almost there. Only go quietly, *sha stil*. If people hear you, they will throw you off the road.

The boys tiptoe silently over to the outpost.

The First Boy	*(laughing)* Oh, it feels so good.
The Second Boy	What feels good? Tell me.
The First Boy	Don't feel anything.
The Third Boy	*Sha*, be still. They'll hear our footsteps.

(pause)

The First Boy	*(laughing)* I'm flying, I'm flying.
The Second Boy	Where? Where?
The Third Boy	*(crying)* Don't leave me alone.

223

The First Boy	Grab on to me. Grab on to me.
The Second Boy	One second, one second.
The Third Boy	*(joyously)* Me too, me too!
All Three	*(shouting)* Oh, how beautiful.
The First Boy	I'm floating around in the clouds. Oh, it is so beautiful! So many blue curtains, and they're billowing like a wind is blowing through them. I'm flying in one and out the other. Oh, I'm chasing after the moon. Oh, how beautiful. Oh Mama!
The Second and Third Boys	Where are you, Yosele, where?
The First Boy	Over here, over here.
The Second and Third Boys	Wait for us, wait for us.
The First Boy	Come with me.
The Second and Third Boys	Where? Where!
The First Boy	Here! Here!
The Second and Third Boys	We're here too. We're here too.
The Second Boy	I see tables covered in so much food.
The Third Boy	With fish and meat.
The First Boy	Not there, go further, go further.

The Second and Third Boys	Where? Where?
The First Boy	Here, here.
The Second Boy	And I see a table, long tables covered in food, everything is delicious. Big loaves of challah on top of challah and women with so many diamonds sitting around the tables. Oh, there is a wedding today or a *bris*. People share a big piece of fish, honey cakes are laid out, now they're cutting them.
The Third Boy	A *bobe* gave me a red apple from the table. Oh, it's so good! A handful of raisins and almonds! Look, I've a full bag of nuts!
The First Boy	Further, hurry, further. There, see, he's riding down from the sky, over the clouds on a white horse, holding a Torah in his hand, with a crown on his head.
The Second and Third Boys	Who? Who?
The First Boy	The Messiah is coming! *Moshiakh!* The Messiah!
The Second and Third Boys	Where? Where?
The First Boy	*(with his last strength)* There, further, further.

The children disappear into the clouds.

The Second and Third Boys	*(crying)* But we see only tables with bread!
The First Boy	*(a voice from the clouds)* Further, further, further.

The boys disappear into the deepest darkness. Dina's figure emerges from the darkness as she moves closer to the road. Yosef, who was waiting for her this whole time, goes to her.

Yosef *(calling to her)* I have been sitting here a long time waiting for you.

Dina *(from the shadows)* My father held me back.

Yosef Everything is ready for the wedding. The *khupe* is raised, the candles are burning already.

Dina *(emerging from the shadows)* I've come. I've come.

She comes completely out of the darkness. Yosef puts his arm around her and walks with her onto the path.

Yosef Arm in arm we go, hand in hand, out of this world and into another.

Dina From bad to good, from unlucky to lucky, from sorrow to joy.

Yosef Step by step we go, standing under a black wedding canopy, memorial candles lighting our path out of this world and into the other.

Dina From chaos to peace.

Yosef To hushed stillness.

Dina What's this around me? I feel like it wants to consume me.

Yosef It is our mother around us.

Dina Our mother?

Yosef The eternal.

(pause)

Dina Why don't I see any light?

Yosef Light is on the other side.

Dina Where?

Yosef Beneath us.

Dina And in front of us?

Yosef Mother darkness herself.

Dina Will it always be like this?

Yosef We are going home.

(pause)

Yosef Take a dream with you from your life for after death so that you will have something to fill the dark days on the other side.

Dina I see only darkness.

Yosef With your last step, from this world into the other, take a dream with you from life for after death.

Dina Where are the dreams?

Yosef Look inside yourself, look for a ray of light, weave together a dream for your dark days.

Dina   I remember nothing from my other life. Everything sinks into the fog, only a few lights appear on the surface, then disappear, they last for a blink of an eye.

Yosef   Grab a light and hold it in front of you. Let it light your last steps.

Dina   I can't go alone. I'm sinking back into the darkness. Help me, Yosef, hold up the light.

Yosef   Only the living can dream. The dead are dead. *(stops)* This is the last blink of your eye, your last step. *(Dina looks inside herself, silent)*

Yosef   Tell me, tell me.

Dina   *(joyfully)* Now I see a light rising up to me.

Yosef   Dream well, dream well.

Dina   I see the *khupe*—candles, girls dancing in a circle around me, raising the *khupe*, the canopy is spread out. The golden threads sparkle around the black silk like fireflies in the night. Right here they're starting to light up; over there they're going out.

Yosef   Dream well, dream well.

Dina   *(as if she wants to remember)* *Klezmorim* play behind the door. My Mama in a new dress carrying the golden tureen over to the table, draped with a white cloth.

Yosef   *(pleading)* Put me into your dream. I am poor and dead.

Dina   *(with joy)* My groom sits next to me with a white shroud draped over his black clothes. I say to him, Yosef, my king!

Yosef Step by step we go under a black wedding canopy, funeral candles light our way out of this world into another.

Dina Hand in hand we go. *Khusn*, you are mine. It is our wedding night tonight, you know.

Dina suddenly stands still, listening to something. From far away we hear voices calling.

Dina My father calls me back.

Yosef Don't look, hold on tight to my hand.

Dina Your hand feels so faint as if it is turning into water. I can barely feel it.

Yosef Hold on to me tight, in the blink of an eye, after one last step, we will be at our destination.

Dina You're disappearing into the air. I don't feel you anymore. Where are you? Where?

Yosef Here beside you, hand in hand, I am going with you.

Dina Who's separating me from you? You're disappearing like in a fog.

Yosef *(pleading with her)* Don't leave me. I am naked and alone.

Dina Who's pulling me away from you? You're disappearing, like a shadow beside me.

Yosef *(becoming fainter and fainter, pleading; we hear only his voice and see a faint sketch of him, like a shadow)* I am poor. I am dead. No one is with me. Only my naked body. Lend me a dream! A little one to take with me into the grave, to light my dark days.

Dina Wait for me. Wait for me.

Yosef How will I fill my dark days, with what?

Dina With longing, like before.

Yosef *(disappearing, says with longing)* O my unlived days! O my un-counted years! O my uneaten bread! My sorrow and my joy lay forgotten in some corner. No one asks about unlived days. No one looks for my uncounted years. They are woven into spider webs.

We hear him weeping.

Dina Why are you crying?

Yosef *(who has disappeared from the night)* Because they slaughtered me so young and sent me away from this world, naked and bare.

Dina *(calling to him)* Be at peace, be at rest.

The fog clears up. The light of dawn. The voices of the villagers grow louder and clearer until the scene is lit and we see the inside of a ruined house as in the second act. Dina lays prostrate in her father's arms, with the women around her. Yosef turns and paces the room by himself.

The First Woman She opened her eyes.

The Second Woman She moved her lips.

The Third Woman She sobbed.

The First Woman The milk saved her.

The Second Woman No, the medicine.

The Third Woman	*(joyful)* She will live, she will live.
Reb Khonen	Praise God! A miracle!

Reb Khonen lays his daughter down on the straw mattress and looks at her.

Yosef	*(comes closer to Dina, with his hands behind him, and asks impassively)* What's happening with the patient?

Everyone looks at him fearfully. No one answers him. Yosef recedes, not getting an answer, starts pacing the room again. The crowd of people avoid him. Everyone looks at him strangely.

The First Woman	Since he showed up among us. *(groans)*
The Second Woman	Why are you surprised? He came to demand what is his.
The Third Woman	*(shocked)* What is his? What do you mean?

Reb Khonen looks at the women in silence.

The Abandoned Wife	Can you believe what she just said!
Second Woman	She knows what I mean.
The Third Woman	What does she mean, what?
The First Woman	You don't see it? Ever since he showed up here there has been so much death around us.
The Second Woman	First he took his mother to that place.
The First Woman	Then Reb Nehemiah, the ox merchant, the widow, and her children.
The Third Woman	How many children?

The First Woman	Everyone who asked him about that other land. He sent all of them to the hill, by the woods, behind the town. Don't you understand? Don't you know what he meant?
The Crowd	What? *Vos?*
The Second Woman	To the cemetery! He sent them to the cemetery!
The Third Woman	*Vey iz undz*, oh the pain, where were our eyes, how could we not see what was happening? What were we thinking?

The crowd looks at Yosef in terror.

The Abandoned Wife	Now can't you see it? He is a dead! Look how he walks.
The Third Woman	*(looking at ailing Dina)* He has come for what is his.
The Second Woman	Taken so early from this world, he can never rest in his grave, *nebekh*.
The Abandoned Wife	It's no so surprise with so many young people taken from this world, lying there in the ground and longing for what is theirs, for what they've lost. They've not lived at all. They're struggling to come back.
The Third Jew	Stupid housewives, what are you saying? The dead come back? Where did you hear that?
The Women	*(pointing at Yosef)* You can see it! The dead come back!
The First Woman	Dragging us with them into the naked grave.
The Second Woman	They demand justice. They demand retribution for their stolen youth.
The Third Woman	What? Will they let us live?

The crowd becomes more and more frightened, looking at each other.

The Abandoned Wife   *(crying out)* Oh no! The dead are coming after us.

The terrified crowd runs into the corners, cowering before Yosef.

Reb Khonen has been listening intently to the women this whole time. He suddenly jumps up from Dina's side and goes over to Yosef, who is separated from the crowd this entire time. Reb Khonen goes right to him, stands in front of him, and looks him in the face.

Reb Khonen   Who are you? Tell me! If you are of the living, stay among the living. But if you are from the dead, go to your eternal rest!

Yosef looks at him with cold eyes and remains standing, not answering. Long pause.

Reb Khonen   *(angrily)* What do you want from us? Why did you come here? We have to start living again.

Yosef looks at Reb Khonen. Yosef shivers and remains silent. Pause.

Reb Khonen   I'll chase you back into your grave with a stick. I'll seal the grave above you myself. Leave us in peace; we must live.

Yosef trembles some more.

Reb Khonen   *(raising his hands to him)* Go back to your eternal rest.

Yosef lumbers off.

SLOW CURTAIN

GLOSSARY

aguna	an abandoned wife who cannot remarry
avade	of course
azoi	so
barukh haShem	blessed be the name of God
bes medresh	study house
bris	circumcision ceremony
bobe	grandmother
gaonim	geniuses
Gemorah	religious text
Gotenyu	Dear God
goyim	gentiles
kaleh	bride
Khumesh	first five books of Bible
khupe	wedding canopy
kind	child
kittel	prayer robe
klezmorim	musicians
khusn	groom
mayn	my
melamed	teacher
mitsve	good deed
Moshiakh	Messiah
nu	so
o va	wow
oy vey iz undz	the pain is upon us
rabbonim	rabbis
sha	quiet
Shabbos	Sabbath
Shavuos	Jewish holiday
Shekhina	feminine presence of God

shtil	quiet
sholem aleichem	greetings, peace be with you
sidur	prayer book
Simchas Torah	holiday celebrating the Torah
talis	prayer shawl
Tatenyu	Dear Father
vos	what
yau	yes

A BIOGRAPHY OF SHOLEM ASCH

A playwright, novelist, short story writer, and journalist, Sholem Asch is one of the most popular Jewish writers in history. Born in Kutno, Poland, in 1880, Asch had a traditional religious Jewish education. When he was nineteen, he moved to Warsaw and began writing in Yiddish under the influence of I. L. Perets and soon thereafter published his first Yiddish work, *Moyshele*, in 1900.

In 1904 he started writing plays, the first of which was *With the Current,* published in 1909 and produced by the Perets Herman Dramatic Studio with Asch in the role of David. His first full length drama, *The Time of the Messiah—A Dream of My People*, was published in Vilna in 1906. This symbolist work was first produced in Russian by the legendary actress-producer Vera Kommisharshevskaya, then in Polish and finally in Yiddish by Jacob Adler in New York City.

In 1907 he introduced his controversial drama about a Jewish brothel owner, *god of vengeance*, which was denounced by many as pornographic. When his mentor the great Yiddish writer I. L. Peretz heard the play at a private reading, he implored Asch to burn it. It was produced by Max Reinhardt's company in Berlin in 1907, opening on Broadway in 1923. The portrayal of Jewish pimps and prostitutes, a lesbian relationship, and the handling of a Torah in the play angered a group of Reform Jews who successfully lobbied for its closing. The company was arrested and convicted of lewd behavior in a widely publicized trial, a decision that was later overturned. The play had previously been performed in tsarist Russia, Sweden, Denmark, Italy, France, Germany, and in Yiddish in New York City without incident.

Asch immigrated to America shortly before World War I and wrote *Der Landsman* (*The Compatriot*), also performed by Julius Adler that year at The Frayer Yidisher Folksbine. *Der Landsman* was the first play produced by the legendary Yiddish company The

Vilna Troupe, which also brought the world S. Anski's play *The Dybbuk*. While in New York, Asch was a writer and editor for the *Jewish Daily Forward*, where many of his novels first appeared in serialized form. A twelve-volume set of his collected works was published in 1922 at the height of his career in the United States. Maurice Schwartz's Yiddish Art Theater, the premier Yiddish repertory company in New York, produced his play *The Dead Man* in honor of that publication after its successful Chicago premiere.

He wrote thirteen full length plays and nine one-acts, including *Night, The Inheritors, The Sinner, Joseph, The Marranos, Winter, Jepthah's Daughter, Shabati Zvi, Amnon and Tamar, Our Faith, A String of Pearls, The Weaklings, Motke Thief, Yikhus, Where Is Father?, The Dead Man, Rabbi Doctor Silver,* and *Coal,* which were all produced by the leading Yiddish acting companies of Eastern Europe and the United States.

Maurice Schwartz dramatized his novels *Three Cities, Kidush ha Shem (The Sanctity of the Name),* and *The Witch of Castille* for popular productions at his Yiddish Art Theater, the longest-running repertory company in New York City's history. Schwartz also made a film of Asch's novel about a sweatshop—*Uncle Moses.* Asch's plays dealt with historical, national, religious, and social issues and are remarkable for their depth of character and daring plots.

Among the actors who starred in the New York Yiddish productions of his plays are Joseph Buloff, Paul Muni, Stella Adler, Jacob Ben Ami, Luba Kadison, Rudolph Schildkraut, David Kessler, Bertha Kalish, David Opatashu, and Jacob Adler. Asch stopped writing for the stage in the late 1920s and focused on his novels, most of which were translated into English. His plays continued to be produced on the Yiddish stages throughout the world, however, and his novels continued to be dramatized up until his death, in 1957.

Among Asch's other novels translated into English are *East River, America, The Mother, Motke the Thief, Uncle Moses, The Prophet, A Passage in the Night,* and *Salvation.* Collections of his short stories in English include *The Children of Abraham* and *From Many Countries; The Collected Short Stories of Sholem Asch.* His work is available in German, Danish, Dutch, Portuguese, Italian, Japanese, Russian, Polish, French, Spanish, Swedish, and Hebrew. Of his two dozen plays only eight have been translated into English and published: the one-acts *Night, The Sinner,* and *Winter* and his full-length dramas *Shabatai Zvi* and *god of vengeance.* Caraid O'Brien has also translated and produced into American English *Motke Thief* and *The Dead Man,* both written in New York City, as well as *On the Road to Zion, Our Faith,* and *A String of Pearls,* which have yet to be staged.

Second only to Bashevis, Asch remains the most translated of Yiddish writers. His trilogy of historical Christian novels—*Mary, The Apostle,* and *The Nazarene*—published in New York between 1939 and 1949, led to an attack by the Jewish press for his inclusion of Christian themes in his work. He was wrongly accused of having converted to Christianity, and a defamatory book was published in Yiddish and English called *The Christianity of Sholem Asch* denouncing his character. Asch responded with the essay "What I Believe," asserting his belief in Judaism and hope for improved Christian-Jewish relations. As a result of the attacks, however, Asch left New York and exiled himself in London and later Israel, where died in 1957. Together with his wife, Madzhe, he had four children—Moses, Nathan, John, and Ruth. His son Moses was the founder of one of the most innovative and culturally significant record labels of the twentieth century, Folkway Records, which he bequeathed to the Smithsonian. Another son, Nathan, was a successful English-language novelist.

CARAID O'BRIEN, TRANSLATOR

Galway-born writer and performer Caraid O'Brien first began learning Yiddish at the Yiddish Book Center in 1994. She graduated from Boston University, phi beta kappa, summa cum laude with a degree in Yiddish literature. She is a three-time recipient of a new play commission from the Foundation for Jewish Culture for her translations of Yiddish plays. She has translated seven plays by Sholem Asch into English, including *god of vengeance, Motke Thief, The Dead Man, On the Road to Zion, Our Faith*, and *A String of Pearls* and is working on her seventh Sholem Asch play, commissioned by Theater J in DC. A 2019 translation fellow at the Yiddish Book Center, Caraid studied Yiddish theater for ten years with Luba Kadison and for six years with Seymour Rexite while performing in the storefront theaters of the Lower East Side, in particular Todo con Nada. For more info visit caraidobrien.com.

AARON BEALL, DRAMATURG

New York native Aaron Beall is the Obie Award–winning co-founder of the New York International Fringe Festival. He ran a series of storefront theaters on the Lower East Side for over a decade, including, most famously, Todo con Nada, which presented 2,500 different productions throughout its history. Additionally, he transformed the infamous Show World strip club into a series of a legit theatrical spaces, beginning with a production of Caraid O'Brien's translation of *god of vengeance*. As an actor he has worked with Julie Taymor, Jim Simpson, and Larry Fessenden.